In Safe Arms

W. Owens

Published by Fantabulous Words

ISBN-13: 978-0-9983093-0-9

DEDICATION

To my wonderful husband, who has put up with me through this whole process. Thank you for being patient while I created. Countless nights of writing, typing, grinning, vetting, laughing, growling, and zoning out paid off.

I finally did it baby!!

ACKNOWLEDGMENTS

To all the ladies who gave me encouragement and ideas to finally make my dream come true of writing for all to see a reality. Thank you for believing I could do it.

To Dana Ellington (Nowata Press Publishing & Consulting), who helped me through the creative process of not giving up and finishing. Celebrating is awesome!

Finally, to my handsome boys, Jordan, Darius, and Damarcus. Every night, you asked me the same question, "Are you finished yet?" Every night I told you the same answer, "No, not yet."

Yes, Mama is FINISHED!

W. Owens

Maxie

Bates General Store was in the middle of 8th Street and Lake with a strip of retail stores reaching down the short block. Inside, it had all the supplies you needed for home improvement. Shelves were lined with paint brushes, screwdrivers, nails, bolts, and anything else you could think of. Even a snack section was there if you needed a quick bite while working up a sweat.

Today, I was on a mission. I grabbed a Phillips screwdriver, glue, and a couple light bulbs. Heading to the checkout, sparkles caught my eye. It was a wind chime with five hummingbirds; two were blue and three were green with yellow wings. Holding them in the air, they made the most beautiful sound and twinkled from the light in the window. I checked the price, nodded my head, and made my way to the front. I knew exactly what I wanted to do with them.

Gil Bates was standing on the other side of the counter. With dark hair sprouting gray at the temples of his tanned skin, the owner still looked young for his sixty-two years. Brown reading glasses sat on the bridge of his narrow nose and a notepad was hanging out of his white, buttoned, short-sleeved shirt. He had a paper in one hand and a pen in the other.

1

"Hey Mr. Bates," I said cheerily placing my things between us.

"Senorita, how is my lovely fairy today?" Mr. Bates had known me since I was six years old and ever since the first day we met, he's called me his lovely fairy. I never knew why but I took to it in smiles every time I heard it, even now as an adult.

"It's a burner out there. I'm trying to get home before everything melts in my car."

"Well let's get you out of here then." As he scanned everything, Mr. Bates lowered his glasses to examine each item.

"And what are you working on today?" he asked.

I looked at him and smiled. He always knew when I came in it meant something happened.

"Just need to fix a lamp I knocked over at my house."

"You know lovely fairy, if you had a handsome fairy on your arm, he could fix your lamp."

I grinned, "Well, if I had a handsome fairy, I wouldn't be able to come visit you and I like coming in here." He placed his hand on his heart thanking me for making his day. Laughing, I grabbed my purchases walking out the door. "Bye Mr. Bates."

I dropped off the bag at my car then walked across the street and down a few buildings to the local grocery mart. I was hoping to be in and out with what I needed, but forty minutes later and with hands full of groceries, I finally made my way to my car out in the sweltering air. Just the short distance caused sweat to bead over my brow and I wondered for the hundredth time why I still lived here in Pine Forest, Texas in this hellish heat.

As I reached the front of my car, I pulled my keys out of my pocket; at the same time, a bag ripped open, spilling everything out. Cursing and opening the door, I put all the other bags inside then bent down to pick up cans and boxes of food off the pavement.

I picked up the last can and put it in my back seat; then I heard loud bangs in the direction of the general store. From across the street, I could see five men run out of the door and get into a dark-colored sedan. The vehicle sped off and in the corner of my eye I could see someone else; Mr. Bates stumbling out of the door with a gun in his hand. I gasped. There was blood all over his white shirt and he was struggling.

I stared in shock as he fired a gun, hitting one of the tires on the car that took off. It lost control and hit the curb so hard and fast, it rocked and landed on its side down the block. Mr. Bates collapsed to the ground.

I grabbed my cell phone and dialed 9-1-1 telling the operator what had just happened.

"Please someone come fast, they shot him and he's not moving! Oh, God!"

"Ma'am where are you and who was shot?"

Mr. Bates was almost motionless, blood pooling around him. The operator told me to go and stay with him until the paramedics came but, I was too scared to go any closer. I rounded my car, got into the driver's side, and looked out my window. He was still breathing, but barely as his head slowly turned my way. Tears streamed down my face because I knew he was helpless and I was there just looking. *I'm sorry, I'm so scared Mr. Bates.* Two men down the street scrambled out of the overturned car and headed back towards us. I stayed completely still and stared across as they made it back to Mr. Bates. One of the men flipped him over as the other man, who was bald with a tattoo on the back of his head, said something then shot him in the head. I screamed and he looked up at me; There was a nasty cut on his face. I started my car and sped off as fast as I could with gunshots following me from the men in the street.

Looking back in my mirror, another car pulled up and the two men got in. I drove like a mad woman down Venit Boulevard, running every light imaginable and trying to keep my distance as far as possible from these people that were quickly closing in. I made a hard left and sped through a neighborhood, then another left.

They were still close behind, and when I looked back again, I noticed that there was smoke coming out the back of my car. I was losing acceleration, which told me that one of the bullets that I heard earlier must have hit something.

Panicking because I was going to have to ditch the car soon, I looked at my surroundings and saw I was near Surpent Park.

I came to a fast stop, jumped out of my car and ran towards the huge park. As I reached the edge of the trees at the front of the entrance, the car that was chasing me pulled up. Turning to look, three men got out and started running after me - the two men from the first car and the driver from the second car. I could see the driver was bald with a mustache and he was wearing slacks and a dress shirt.

"Don't let her get away," someone said behind me. I had enough distance that I would be able to lose them once I got further into the trees. Paths ran in all directions for the public and it was easy to get off track for those who were not familiar with the area. Big river birch and weeping willow trees layered five acres of land. Only one trail led you to a fish pond in the middle of it all and the rest took you eventually out of the park. I was on the path to the pond.

I knew exactly where I was going because I used to spend hours with my friends exploring every nook and cranny of this place when I was younger. We thought we were nature guides so we did everything we thought they did, climbing trees, picking plants and leaves and making our own little pretend campsite. If you were ever looking for us outside of our house, we were here at Surpent Park having an adventure.

Running for what seemed like hours as hard as I could, I moved through trees and bushes, leaves and twigs slapped my face and scratched my skin. I ended up making it up and over a hill surrounded by brush that was deep within the park, I instinctively got on all fours and moved branches to the side with my lungs on the verge of exploding. I was never more excited to see what I saw at that moment. It was a small space on the other side of the hill that was well hidden from all the plants that grew around it. The Cave, as we called it, was what my friends and I used as a secret hideaway when we wanted to have girls only meetings.

The ground was covered in moss and dirt, spider branches reached out in all directions. It had been years since I had been here but it looked almost exactly the same as back then. Dark, dank, but safe, I scrambled on my hands and knees as fast and as far as I could inside. In my haste, my wrist rolled underneath the weight of my body and a branch ripped my skin viciously below my left shoulder. I cried out in pain then covered my mouth with my other hand to muffle the sound so no one could hear me. I didn't realize my phone had been in my hand the whole time and it showed 911 was still on the line. Huffing hard, I used my good arm to talk in the receiver. Trembling and in agony, I spoke hoarsely in the earpiece.

"Please... Help me! I'm at..." The signal went out. I tried to reach up for more bars so I could call back but it was in and out. Tears streamed down my face when I realized it was no use. Shaking, I put the phone on silent so I didn't lead anyone in my direction and slid my location device on. Putting the phone in my lap, I waited and waited, praying help was on the way soon.

♫

The searing pain was excruciating and I could feel warm liquid running down my arm. Because it was so dark, I couldn't see it but I knew I didn't want to; the pain put a picture in my mind of how bad it was. I didn't think my wrist was broken but I knew something was wrong because of the swelling I felt. It had been quiet for some time outside of the small shelter and it was getting cold. The shivering didn't help the pain so I was tempted to leave but hesitated every time I heard anything. I was hopeful the police had to be coming for me soon because they could track me, but as time passed, I started to worry.

Lots of sounds started coming from the left of where I was. I went completely still as it got louder and louder, my body shaking in fear. I could hear shuffling and yelling, but I couldn't see anything so I pulled out my phone and turned on the flashlight. Looking around I saw a small opening right above my head and I positioned my body to see out. The two men from the street were out there and it looked like they were fighting someone, only it didn't look like a jogger and it wasn't the other guy from the car. He had on black clothes, a bullet proof vest, and gun in a holster on his hip. One of the guys tried to come from behind to hit him with a large branch, but the man kicked him in the stomach and sent him to the ground. The other man pulled out a gun, fired and missed just as the man in black hit the hand holding it. One blow to the chin from the officer stopped the man in his tracks and he hit the ground with a thud. I could hear shouting in the distance and suddenly officers swarmed the area with guns out.

I noticed the man who was fighting the two guys standing with his hands on his hips breathing heavily. An officer was speaking to him and he was pointing from the direction they came from. The men who were after me were hauled off and everyone else followed except the man wearing black. He was looking on the ground for something, then pulled up a phone from the dirt. He suddenly paused and looked around quickly, resting his eyes in my direction then running over. I was so out of it by then and in shock, I didn't even realize I had been yelling for help. The willow branches were peeled open from the front with light shooting in. Making his way halfway inside, I was face to face with the man who saved me.

"It's ok, you're safe now, take my hand." I looked down at my arm and wrist. My whole arm was streaked with blood and my wrist was the size of a baseball. He followed where my eyes went and crawled in further. His large body covered the entrance and light burst through more holes as the officer used his hands to make a bigger clearance to get me out. The safe place of secrets, and stories, and girl gossip turned into a place that kept me alive and out of harm's way and I was thankful. Once outside, I was able to stand straight up but I felt very dizzy and nauseous; the adrenaline was wearing off. The man looked at me with concern and I was trying to speak but the words tumbled out. I had no idea what I was saying. He picked me up with one swift movement just as I close to fainting. My head lagged on his shoulder, I whispered, "Please don't leave me."

Lance

Lance Tillis, Special Services Operative for the Federal Government Agency, was the first to arrive at the crime scene. He had been investigating the Meek organization for the past year for drug trafficking and illegal firearm dealings. After his last visit to New Mexico on a tip, Lance had gathered enough information to find the head associate who handled shipments for the firearms in the small town of Pine Forest, Texas. He knew the location of where the meetings took place and the name of the person heading it all, Gil Bates, who had been an acquaintance of Meek's for two years. Lance was on his way to run surveillance for the third time in three weeks when he heard police chatter about a shooting in the vicinity, the victim being Gil Bates.

Lance arrived at the scene within twenty minutes and took a survey of the area. A body was in the middle of the main street, a man in his late 60's, a gunshot wound to his chest and head. Looking down at the corpse, he could ID Gil Bates. He spoke with the medical examiner briefly then started down towards the end of the block. Officers on scene were already processing evidence at the wrecked car and had removed three bodies from it. Looking at each person, he knew without a doubt they were Meek members because they each had a tattoo of a spider on their hand.

Walking up to the back of the car, Lance kneeled. Dried blood on the ground from near the sedan indicated someone managed to get out because it didn't connect with the bodies taken out and it was advised a door was open when officers arrived at the scene. Lance followed the trail of blood to Gil Bates, then another trail set about five feet away that lead to tire tracks. He could see two sets of tire marks within thirty feet of one another. His brow furrowed as he went to inspect them both. The treads from the sets were different from one another, but fresh.

"According to a 911 dispatcher, a woman called in saying she witnessed a shooting," a plain clothes officer said walking up to Lance. "They stayed on the line until shortly before you arrived when the call was dropped. The woman was trying to tell them where she was. We haven't been able to reach her again, but our hunch is the call is related to this here."

Lance looked at the tire marks again. They didn't appear to be brake lines; they looked more like someone speeding off. Something was definitely wrong here. Another officer rushed to Lance.

"The cellphone location device is activated. Calls have been coming in that a car was driving down Venit Boulevard at a high rate of speed, and another car was behind it doing the same."

"I need GPS coordinates now. Someone is still out there going after this witness. I need to get to them before they get to her, or we'll have another crime scene."

Rushing to his car and leaving the scene, Lance was hoping to run into something before it was too late. He was given all the information from the witnesses' phone. It had been stationary for a while and he didn't want to expect the worst. Because Lance wasn't familiar with this city he was hoping there were clues to help get to the location quicker.

The marker he received was leading to a huge park about five minutes in front of his current location. As he came up to the area, there was a car parked at an odd angle at the curb with the driver door open. Another car was right behind it and had three doors opened. Hoping he wasn't too late, he pulled up right behind the car and jumped out with his gun raised after calling in that he'd found the vehicles.

The first car he approached had blood in the back-passenger seat which indicated someone was hurt and, more than likely, was the person whose blood had been left from in front of the store. Lance walked around, then looked over at the other car; it appeared empty. As he walked up to it, he noticed there was a bullet hole in the gas tank. Opening the back door, he saw bags of groceries scattered about. Looking down, there were blood drops on the pavement along with a set of fresh tire tracks that lead west.

Lance looked at the GPS and the pink ping flashing back at him. He raced into the park as fast as he could. After ten minutes of searching and being surrounded by trees, the tracking on the phone showed she was just over a small incline in what looked like an open space, but he could hear voices and movement to the right.

W. Owens

Maxie

I had been in the hospital for almost two days with a nasty cut on my arm and a sprained wrist. The doctors said it looked worse than it really was and I would be fine in no time. They gave me twenty stitches, a sling to keep my arm up, and a wrap for my wrist. Because it was all on the left side, it made it easier, but it still sucked.

Sleeping was just about nonexistent; people were coming in and out of the room all morning, including officers to take my statement. I hadn't been in the mood to tell them anything anymore after the first day; I just wanted answers. Who those guys were that gunned down Mr. Bates? Was I safe? No one seemed to know anything, or I should say, tell me anything and that made me uncomfortable. I wanted to go home.

At 11am my hospital room door opened and in came a man that looked vaguely familiar. He was about 6 ft. 2, with very broad shoulders under a dark blue shirt covered a very obvious muscular physique. I could see a tattoo of a cobra on his forearm. He was wearing black cargo pants with a gun holster fastened to it. His skin reminded me of hazelnut cappuccino and his eyes were the same light color brown as mine but they looked surprisingly soft from his hard-outer shell. A neatly faded haircut was about as thin as his nicely trimmed beard over a solid square jawline. The man was, as my Gram would say, "Finer than your Sunday Best."

"Hello, Ms. McHill. Do you remember me from the park?" he spoke deeply. It took me a moment but it finally came to me; the man in the park who saved me.

"Yes, I don't remember your name, though, sorry."

"I probably would not have remembered either. I'm Lance Tillis with the FGA. You can call me Lance if you like."

I smiled back and extended my hand. "You can call me Maxie." He sat down to the right of me in a chair and moved it closer to my bed. I shifted my body to face him and tried to adjust the pillow in my lap propping up my arm. Lance grabbed and fixed it for me, gently lifting my arm and placing it on the pillow. He definitely wasn't like the officers that had been visiting me for sure, those guys would have just looked at me. He had a certain demeanor about him that I was drawn to. I grabbed his arm before he moved away.

"I never got to say thank you...for everything. I'm very grateful."

"You're welcome Maxie." He smiled warmly then cleared his throat and sat in his chair leaning a little further. I could tell something was up the way his body vibed.

"I wanted to talk to you about what happened two days ago and what is going on right now."

"I'm glad somebody wants to. No one seems to want to tell me anything. I was starting to get pissed off."

Lance went in to explain his job as an Operative for FGA and what he had been doing for the past year investigating a group called Meek. He said they were trying to get them on a lot of charges for guns, drugs and even kidnapping and murder to put them away for a long time. They had been getting evidence so they had enough to send this case to a federal judge and get charges filed as soon as possible. Lance told me that Mr. Bates was actually one of the main contacts for transporting everything and it was two days ago that a shipment was scheduled to go out of the docks.

"You're kidding, right? You must be talking about a different Mr. Bates because that's just plain crazy." There was no way he had the right person. This is the same man who gave out quarters to the kids who came into his store, and the same man who called me his lovely fairy. *Mr. Bates was working with men who sold guns and drugs, not possible.*

"I don't believe it," I said shaking my head. "I've known Mr. Bates since I was a little girl, he wouldn't do anything like that, he just wouldn't. You might want to check your sources." Lance handed me three photos from a yellow envelope he brought in the room.

"This picture was taken one month ago." Mr. Bates was shaking hands with someone that had their back turned to the camera. He was in front of a huge crate in the back of his storage room at the general store. The one thing I noticed was that he wasn't smiling, and Mr. Bates always smiled. The second picture showed him standing to the side while a different man was holding a package that looked duct taped. The third picture had Mr. Bates putting an envelope it in his front pocket of his plaid shirt. My heart sank and I sat back on the bed, there was no denying those pictures. *I never would have thought in a million years, that someone as kind-hearted as him…*

"I know this is a blow to you, but our group has been after this organization for some time now. FGA is very thorough, he definitely was involved and I can say that with one hundred percent certainty." He opened up a notebook and grabbed a pen from his cargo pants.

"I know you had no idea of Mr. Bates activities, but can you think back and tell me if there has been anything that has ever struck you as odd about him?" Still trying to get past what I just heard, I tried to get my mind reeling backward. He never ever gave any inkling to me or anyone else that I could think of that he would be a person like that. With a small town like this, if something was weird with him, everyone would have known.

"There isn't much to tell about him, he was always warm, like the town dad you know. I mean even when I was a teenager he told me how I reminded him of his…daughter…A daughter that he didn't talk much about, but when he did, he would get real sad. I never asked him what happened to her." Lance scribbled on his notepad then looked up and nodded.

"We do know that he has family in Mexico and they have been trying to get papers and money to make it to the states. I can only guess that he was doing this to bring them over, but FGA is still looking into it. The men you saw the other day were the runners. I'd say that if they came in the store like that, something must have gone wrong with the shipment deal." Lance put the pen down and looked at me.

"Is there anything else you can think of about Mr. Bates." I shook my head no. To tell me that someone I've known all my life was crooked, I would never see anything about him as bad.

"If anything comes up to your mind, please let me know."

"Ok."

Lance glanced over at the door to the room then looked back at me.

"I'm sure you've noticed the armed guard outside your door by now." I nodded looking in the direction of the door and saw the top of the guards' head.

"That is for your protection for the time being until you get out of here. From there a US Marshall will take over."

"Why? What's happening?" I sat up in my bed, panic covering my face. I'm not sure if he wasn't supposed to tell me or just didn't want to tell me, in either case, something was wrong when I saw his expression.

"What the hell is going on? Why do I think you aren't telling me everything?" Lance put the pen and notebook on the nearby table and leaned his arms on his thighs.

"About two years ago, FGA raided an old abandoned restaurant on the border of Mexico and Texas from a tip of an inside drug informant. They were given information that a big sale was set to take place between a new group on the scene and some old local dealers. What FGA didn't know was the newbies who called themselves Meek, set up the old dealers to kill and steal all the merchandise-cocaine and firearms."

"Damn," I said. Lance nodded.

"Our informant was able to give us some reliable information that this new group, Meek, was trying to be the only organization to run in the area and had pretty much succeeded. We tried to run background on the group for quite a while and found a lot of useful information on them."

"Like what?"

"For starters, we knew that from the carnage they left at the restaurant, they meant business. This wasn't some one-time deal in their favor, their endgame is being on top. There doesn't look to be a lot of leaders but from what we can tell, orders seem to be coming from one source. They stay pretty hidden in location so it has been difficult to find exact whereabouts of their main operation site. Fortunately for us, we did get pictures of some group members so we were hoping we could catch a lead from following some of them."

Lance pulled out pictures and explained to me that some of these were the men at the scene as well and in the park. He also gave me a little background on them and their current status. Two were arrested and three were deceased due to the car that flipped from Mr. Bates shooting at it. I studied each picture, no one looked familiar, but I thought to what he said. *Two arrested and three deceased, there was something bothersome about that number.* My mind stayed wrapped on that until I realized what it was that didn't make sense.

"This isn't all of them." Frowning, Lance looked down at the pictures then back to me.

"What do you mean?"

I pointed to the pictures in my lap, "If these are all the men you have, then you better get people looking around because there's a guy missing. There were five guys that went into the store and when the car crashed only two guys got out. Another car pulled up and they all got in and chased me to the park." I continued, "There's another man out there."

"Shit," Lance said under his breath. He quickly looked again at the pictures then put everything back in the envelope and stood up. He looked at me and I swear I saw his face flash some concern.

"With all this being said, we really have to keep close watch on you to make sure…"

"Make sure what?" I said cutting him off in alarm. Lance paused for a moment before speaking.

"To make sure no one comes after you." That one sentence alone freaked me out. *It's not over, they might still come after me?*

"I need to call my parents; they need to know," I said shakenly.

"It's best you don't let anyone know right now, for their safety and yours.

"You're scaring me. What kind of trouble have I gotten into?"

The reality of everything sent my blood pressure monitor off. Lance came close just as a nurse rushed in, checked the monitor, ran vitals and advised me to try to relax. She left the room, eying Lance suspiciously as he slowly approached my bed.

"Are you ok?" he asked. I looked at him and didn't say a word. *How the hell did he think I was? You don't just come in and tell someone that a group of bad people might try to come and kill you.* He might not have said they would kill me, but he might as well have. Lance handed me a cup of water from the table and I hesitantly took it from him, taking small sips. He placed a hand gently on my shoulder.

"I'm sorry, I didn't mean to make you feel that way. What I should have said was we have to follow all protocols for a situation like this and we will contact your parents once we get a clearer picture of things, ok?" I sat there holding the cup and looked around the room; my hand was still trembling a little.

"When will you be able to leave and go home?" Lance asked suddenly. I looked at him puzzled. "Probably this afternoon, why?" He got up and moved to the door looking back at me.

"I'll be back before then." With that, he left and I sat there feeling my blood pressure rise again as tears slid down my face. I was scared and alone and couldn't tell anyone what was happening. I didn't know what to do.

♬

It was pretty late in the afternoon and I was exhausted. From the time Lance left I cried, and I'm not a crybaby, but all this going on had me a mess. I didn't want the nurses to see me like that because all I needed was for them to tell me I had to stay longer for observation. Once the last nurse came in to tell me I could leave, I was trying to figure out how I could get a ride home since I wasn't supposed to talk to anyone, but fortunately Lance came back before I decided to call a cab. Even though I could walk on my own two feet, it was protocol to be wheeled out in a chair to leave.

They didn't take me to the main entrance of the hospital, instead, I was taken through the employee exit on the backside of the hospital. I felt like I had Secret Service permissions with Lance bringing up the rear as the nurse led the way. I always thought it would be fun to get special treatment like celebrities do, with bodyguards, and I get to go here and there and no one else could. It's wasn't fun and it actually scared the shit out of me because this wouldn't be paparazzi following me around to get close, it would be people trying to hurt me.

Warm heat blasted my face as soon as we stepped outside and the nurse pushed me up to the curb. I looked around and noticed we were next to the employee parking lot. There were two nurses at a table talking and eating, not paying any attention to us. Three other tables sat empty except for a few birds that had flown down to pick up crumbs. Other than the nurses and us, no one else was out there.

We had to wait a couple minutes so Lance could pull up his ride. It was a real nice charcoal colored Ford Explorer. From the outside, you would think it was just a regular SUV. Once he helped me get into the front, I knew there was nothing regular about it. Right in front of me above the glove box was a screen with a small keyboard underneath it. Another screen was on the middle console and was swung facing Lance. The GPS and radio were where they would normally be but there were all kinds of buttons and things all over.

I looked behind me and in the second row, in the center, was another screen with a keyboard. The only thing that looked normal was the third-row seat, but that was because all I could see was the tops of the seats and black bags. I sat back and looked out the tinted windows. *If he ever got deserted anywhere, he'd be ok. He probably had a fridge and bed back there too.*

"Thanks for bringing me home, I appreciate it," I finally said as we started down the road. Lance looked over at me and smiled warmly. I noticed he had deep dimples that creased his face.

"You are welcome." I looked out and rolled down the window halfway, feeling the fresh air on my face. The summer heat in Pine Forest was in full effect, most people with air conditioners stayed inside until the evenings but I loved the heat unless it was close to melting my face. Moments like that was when I wished I lived up north.

"Now I have your address but you will have to direct me because I don't know too much about the residential areas."

"Ok. Turn left at the next light."

I instructed him to keep straight for two miles then merge onto the expressway. I didn't speak much the rest of the trip besides directing him to my place. I didn't feel like making small talk, I just wanted to get home.

My townhouse was in the middle of a small gated community. Ten brick buildings lined one side and five lined the other. Each building was two stories high, the corner units had narrow balconies for a couple of chairs and maybe a small table. A small walkway stood between each unit and it walked back into a small patio. Bushes lined the sidewalk and because we were in a covenant community, gardeners kept the plants and yards up. My front yard was about ten feet long, and eight feet wide; a sidewalk took you right to my front door. I had Lance drive around to the back-alley entrance so no one could see me since I had a sling and a brace on. Nothing like nosy neighbors when you don't need them.

Lance got out first and grabbed my hospital bag from the back seat. As he was coming around to my side, I realized I was hungry, then I realized something else…groceries!

"Son of a bitch!" I exclaimed as Lance opened the door to the truck for me.

"What's wrong?" he asked.

"I had food in my car, like I just finished shopping when this happened. Do you think they took it out? It's been days."

"I really don't know but I can try and find out. They were going to drop it off at the impound when they were done," Lance responded as I was heading up to the door.

"The impound? Are they crazy? Do you know how much that's gonna cost? Why can't they just drop it off here?" He shut the truck door.

"I'll talk to them and see if we can have it sent here, but if they already put it in impound, you won't be charged for it. That's standard not to leave evidence in the same place when it's done being looked over."

I took my keys out and opened the back door. Walking straight through the place through the front, we came into a small living room. A window was next to the door with a T.V. stand in front of it and directly across from that was a couch and coffee table with a stress fountain on top. Water lightly trickled through rocks that ran along its journey to the bottom of the stones. Each rock had a word engraved on it; *live, love, joy, create, believe, encourage.* Two huge spider plants were potted in corners of the room and I had a small china cabinet with glass figurines inside on one wall.

I had Lance put my things in the living room and have a seat while I walked around the small townhome inspecting everything. Beyond the couch was the staircase that lead up to my room. I had a full-sized bed, two night stands with lamps on them and a huge dresser drawer. Artwork of music notes covered my walls.

Back downstairs and to the right was a small room that held my grandmother's piano in the center. Sheet music covered the top and a small settee sat in front of my window in the corner. A tall bookshelf was along the wall with hundreds of records, tapes and CDs. Out of that room and to the left was my kitchen. There was an island in the middle with a deep sink and long countertop with two tall chairs that posed as my kitchen table. If you sat and looked across from the chairs, the oven range and the fridge sat with a few cabinets running alongside it.

Satisfied everything looked good, I adjusted my sling and grabbed bottled water for the both of us. Seeing as my food was nearly nonexistent before the incident and nothing about that changed, I had to get to the store somehow. Walking back into my living room, Lance was standing at the big window looking out. I handed him a water.

"Thanks," he said. I reached in my hospital bag pulling out a pill bottle. I was thankful I relented when the doctor gave me the pain pills even though I didn't want them because my wrist was throbbing. Lance came and sat down on the far end of the couch.

"How long do you have to have the sling on?"

"Um, the doctor said a couple days since there was a little damage. Doesn't want me to bust a stitch before they're ready to come out, though. Gotta keep the brace on the wrist for a couple of weeks." I looked down at it and frowned.

"I'll be here for a while to help with the investigation so if you need any help with anything just let me know. I'll leave my card with you." I thought about my car at the impound and how since I can't talk to anyone for the moment it was going to be hard to get things done so I probably would need help after all. His phone rang and looking down at the number, he answered it.

"Tillis." He was silent a moment then stood up. I decided to give him a little privacy and walked in the kitchen again so I could take inventory of what I needed to get for food. After I counted fruit, vegetables, meat and bread, I went to a magnetic notepad with a pen on the fridge and started making a list. I could still hear Lance talking in the living room and kept writing. Looking up and to the window, I noticed my small fern in the sill was droopy.

26

"Hey there, let me get you something to drink little one." I whispered. I filled up a quarter cup of water and an ice cube to pour in the plant. Then, taking one last look at my list and looking around, I left the kitchen and headed out and in the living room.

"Ok, sir. Thank you… bye." Lance ended the call and turned to look at me. He had an odd expression on his face that told me once again something was up. I sat on the couch eyeing him.

"That was my superior with an update. I think you met him in the hospital." I nodded remembering the big burly white guy with the receding hairline and gruffy voice.

"So given the circumstance of this particular case and the fact that there is still one man not in custody that was involved, he would like me to keep my eye on you until further notice." I nodded my head in understanding.

"Well that makes sense, I can see being watched over from time to time."

Lance shook his head, "No, not surveillance. He wants me to keep my eye on you 24-7." I frowned in confusion.

"As in stay here with you 24-7," he said. I sat up where I was.

"What the hell?!" I was in utter shock. *Have they lost their mind? They want me to let this man I don't even know stay in my place and watch me.*

"This is just a safety precaution until the chief feels comfortable."

"Well how long before he feels comfortable?" *Here I was just getting home and now this.*

"He's not sure…" I stood up.

"Of course he isn't sure, nobody knows nothin, right." I started pacing the floor but my head began to spin. I wobbled a little and Lance was over in a split second.

"I'm good, I'm good, just a little dizzy from the medicine." I sat down and held my head with my hands. "I need to process this," I said. We were both silent for some time. I'm sure he wasn't expecting this either so I couldn't be mad at him, but I could be mad at that boss of his. I drew in a deep breath and blew air out. This was beginning to be the pits, and I wanted it to go away but I knew it wouldn't.

"Ok, I'm not happy about this at all."

"I understand."

"I'm pretty ticked off."

"I'm sorry," Lance replied. I brushed my hand in the air thinking how this day got so much better, so much freakin' better.

"Ya'll do what ya'll need to do." I didn't mean to have the attitude behind what I said but I did and it lingered in the air for a while. My privacy was about to be invaded by a stranger, he was nice and all, but he was a stranger. Lance looked at the time and glanced back over to me.

"I need to grab some things out of my truck."

"Whatever, I'll get you a blanket and a pillow. Couch is your bed, it folds out." I walked out the room as Lance stood there for a moment then went through the kitchen to the back door. I was over everything now as I felt an attitude coming on as I climbed the stairs to get the blanket and pillow from the closet. I felt bad about treating him like I did but I was too through. I felt like nothing good was happening and it should have been by now. I turned to head back downstairs and bumped into the wall. I hadn't eaten anything which was probably why I felt like such a lightweight at the moment from the pain pills. The door opened back up and I called out to Lance. He came to the bottom of the stairs and slowly started to climb up.

"Here's your stuff, I'm gonna go lay down okay?"

"Are you good?" Lance asked as I realized the wall had been holding most of my body up.

"I just wanna lay down." He walked up to me and lead me to my room and I didn't protest. Once in there, I laid on the bed and he propped my slinged arm on a pillow. That's the last thing I remembered; I was probably sleep within seconds.

When I opened my eyes, moonlight spilled through the window. I blinked a couple of times then sat up and looked around realizing where I was and yawned. I climbed out of bed to head downstairs. I could see Lance sitting on the couch with a laptop in his lap and I realized nothing from earlier was the dream I thought it was.

"How long was I sleep?" I asked, taking the last step down. He looked at his watch.

"About two hours." I stayed standing behind the couch, thinking back earlier and how I was acting. He really didn't deserve the 'tude' I gave him.

"So look, I'm sorry about earlier. I was irritated and my mind was a little cloudy." He looked at me and nodded in understanding. I told him I didn't have much food in the house but I could make a couple sandwiches. Lance typed a couple more things then closed his laptop and followed me into the kitchen.

"I was looking at all your entry and exit points. You don't have an alarm system."

"I never thought about getting one, I guess I should now." I walked over and opened the fridge. Ham, cheese, mustard and mayo were placed on the cutting board that was fitted on top of my countertop. With one hand, I was able to make two sandwiches, but I asked Lance to open the bag of chips on top of the fridge. We sat at the counter with our food.

"That's a nice piano in your spare room."

"Thanks, it was my Gram's...It was passed on to me when she died. She knew how much I loved it."

I started thinking of everything that's happened so far and felt depressed. *I witnessed a murder, got chased, then got rescued. My car was who knows where and I had stitches and a sprained wrist. I couldn't call anyone to talk to them about what happened and I'm in my house eating with a man I barely knew, who has to stay here constantly until who knows when. If I could drink my sorrow away right now I would in a heartbeat, until I passed out on the floor.* Lance interrupted my thoughts.

"Your car is going to be brought tomorrow in the morning." I got up and stacked our empty plates with my one good hand. Lance took them from me and headed to the sink.

"You don't have to do that," I said.

"Your arm still needs to rest, it's fine." He found the dish soap and sponge then washed and dried the dishes. I eased back on the stool holding my wrist and thought to myself that was nice of him to do that, but I was still not happy about all of it.

"Thank you."

"You're welcome." He finished with the dishes then sat back on the stool next to me.

"I understand this is overwhelming, all of this. I wasn't expecting it either, but if the chief thinks this is in the best interest, then I need to follow orders on this one." I stared down at the counter, I knew inside he was right, but it was a lot to handle.

"So he is sure this is the only way?"

"Yes."

"This group is that bad?" He nodded. I thought back to what he's told me about them, and it was a scary thought to imagine now. The more my mind went there, the more I was beginning to feel relieved Lance was here. I glanced around my tiny place sighing.

"My space is really small, but you should have enough room for whatever you need. Maybe tomorrow after the car gets here, you can take me to the store so we don't starve."

"Sure."

"I know you kind of walked around earlier but I'll show you around." I lead him through the whole townhouse. I only had a half bathroom downstairs so he would have to use the upstairs bathroom in my room to shower. I showed him where to put his laptop up if he didn't want to leave it on the coffee table. I walked with Lance to every door and window and he made sure they were all locked up. Afterward, he went into the kitchen to make a call to the chief and I walked into the spare room with Gram's piano. I ran the keys over with my good hand and sat down in front of it.

"Well Gram, you said it best, "If it ain't rained cats and dogs, it ain't rained yet." I leaned my head forward and rested it on the top where I placed my music sheet. I softly tapped the keys lazily like I always did when I was troubled. It always made me feel better because it took me back when I was little and Gram would play songs for me. Sometimes I would tap the keys while she played. She never stopped me, she just kept playing and smiling and I kept tapping. I sure did miss her.

W. Owens

Lance

Lance saw the beautiful woman in the hospital bed noticeably uncomfortable. The expression on her face was imprinted in his mind, terrified and confused. She had smooth brown skin and brown oval eyes. Her wavy jet black hair was pulled back into a loose bun, small tendrils framing her face. He could tell that she hadn't slept much due to the circles under her eyes, but yet she was breathtaking and he had to blink to keep from staring. There was work to do, lots of work.

When Maxie explained in her light southern drawl to him that there were three men that chased her and not just the two that were in custody, Lance knew he needed to make some moves quick. It would only be a matter of time before word got out that there was a witness who could possibly ID people in the organization; she would no longer be safe.

Lance knew that her being involved as a witness to a crime was one thing, but being a witness to a crime like murder was on a much bigger level, especially if so far she is the only person to have seen everything go down as no one else has come forward with a report. He knew keeping her safe was going to be difficult because he was certain Meek wasn't going to just lie lightly on this.

With the chief calling Lance and telling him that he was assigning him to protective status for Maxie, he was relieved but disturbed at the same time. This changed everything drastically because, by the chief acknowledging Lance's concern for her, it stamped his reservations about leaving her alone, especially since at the present time, she wasn't one hundred percent.

Speaking with the chief, he asked for a timeframe and if FGA would consider putting Maxie in Witness Protection after formal charges were set for the two men in the park. They had been looking into that as well as talking about keeping Lance in the protection program with her instead of assigning another officer since he had pretty much been with her from the beginning. If the chief wanted him to think about going to a safe house with Maxie, it really meant he needed to go to the safe house with her.

There were a number of things that needed to be done soon. He would need to ensure that he kept her in sight as much as possible. Lance did not want to smother Maxie, but given the importance of keeping her safe, he had to take certain precautions. He needed to gather as much information as possible on Maxie McHill in order to make this transition all work and stay a step ahead of Meek at all times.

Maxie

I slept decently that first night home, mostly due to the medicine the hospital gave me. Once daylight starting streaming through my window, I was wide awake, after laying there for a while, I showered carefully then came back into my room wrapped in a towel. Sitting on the bed with wet hair down my back, I tried to peel my bandage off my arm so I could clean up the stitched up cut and let it air out before covering it again. Pulling it slowly wasn't working because I could feel every hair being torn from my arm so I bit my lip and decided to rip it off as fast as I could, hoping the pain would be minimal.

"Mmmmm!" I cried out and held my arm. Tears blurred my vision and I had to wait a second cause I wasn't expecting it to hurt so bad. Who would have thought taking a band aid off would be such agony, and I only managed to peel half of it off. I heard footsteps, then Lance burst through the door with his gun drawn. I gasped and held the towel around me tight trying to cover my body. Seeing the gun pointing at me drained all the color from my face, I was frozen in fear. It felt like I could see right down it to the bullet in the chamber. Lance lowered his weapon and apologized over and over again coming over to me but stopping mid-way noticing what he walked into.

I pointed to the bandage still halfway on my arm, trying to steady myself while waving him away. Lance stood a second longer then backed out and closed the door. My heart was beating out my chest, I wasn't expecting to be face to face with a gun in my room. It took me a minute or two to calm down and take some deep breaths. I looked down and saw the bandage still hanging and I ripped the rest of it off, wincing. I managed to calm down enough to put on some clothes and put the wrap on my wrist with the sling. Looking at myself in the mirror I took long deep breaths then went out my door. *It was just Lance, no one else, just Lance, you're ok.*

Downstairs, Lance was sitting on the couch leaning forward, his hands clasped together. He stood up when I entered.

"I'm really sorry."

"Maybe next time ask me if I'm ok before busting in." I stood there looking at him closely. Lance looked remorseful and I began to feel a little bad for him.

"Well, at least I know no one would get in here without you hearing. That's a good thing." He looked back at me with a little less worry.

"What an ice breaker," he mumbled embarrassed at his actions.

"Walking in on a stranger in a towel...yep, I'd say so." I think I saw him turn a shade of red even with his darker skin. I decided to change the subject because it was just as uncomfortable for me as it was for him.

"So look, I got a towel, cloth, paste and soap up there. The water should be fine, go on up there so you can freshen up." He went to walk past me, then stopped. Lance looked at my arm then reached over and adjusted my sling.

"You have it too high, you should be able to hang your arm comfortably in it when you wear it." He stopped touching it when I stared at him. Now speechless, Lance walked up the stairs and into my room to the bathroom. I stared after him silently. *This day is already starting to be weird.*

Our morning breakfast consisted of sausage links and coffee. Once again, we sat in silence eating, not knowing what to say. Lance eventually grabbed his laptop and I just sat there thinking with a second cup of joe to my lips. I really needed to get to the store. I needed to call work…

I heard what sounded like a truck pull up in the back alleyway. My garage was detached from the townhouse so the kitchen had a door that walked out to it. Lance stood up then told me to follow him out. Together, we headed through the door and small patio. There was a small gate that opened up to the alley.

Tate's Towing was there with my car on the bed. A short Hispanic guy with a long ponytail jumped out the front. He came around to greet us with a clipboard in his hand.

"Maxie McHill?"

"Yes, sir."

"I jus need you to sign this paper and you good to go." I looked it over and signed then walked to the garage door and put in the code to raise it as he began to lower my car and talk to Lance. I came back just as he threw the clipboard in the cab.

"I reckoned you not let the Missus see the inside in the back, it's none too purty."

"Missus?" I called out. The driver shook hands with Lance gave him my keys and climbed back up into his truck to drive off.

Taking the keys from him, I opened up the door. Fumes of rotted food entered my nostrils. I gaged and took a step back.

"Holy shit!" Lance looked through the open door.

"They didn't have the decency to throw it out. Oh, I can't believe it." I turned away and walked back in my house, grabbing trash bags and rubber gloves, cursing the whole way back out. Lance grabbed a bag and put it next to my car. He started pulling stuff out and into the open bag. I grabbed all the non-food items and put them in another bag. When all the things were out, all the windows were rolled down and the car was put in the garage. He took the full trash bag and put it outside the garage in the large can. We walked back into the house, where I washed my hands until they were almost red.

"Bullshit this is, can't even take the damn food out the goddamn car." I mumbled angrily drying my hands.

"I'll let the chief know about this, that is unacceptable."

"You damn straight that's unacceptable. Why the hell would they leave that? You tell them they better hope to Jesus that smell comes out cause they don't want me to go straight the hell off. They don't know me."

And that was the truth, they didn't know me. Maxie Ann McHill was a firecracker when she was mad with a hot fuse. If I need to, I'll tell you off and won't blink. My daddy told me I was his little spitfire because I might look sweet and approachable, but don't get on my wrong side because I can hold my own. When I get in a mood I tend to keep the attitude longer than I need to and with that comes a stronger southern accent that says 'don't go there with me'. Most people haven't had the pleasure of hearing it, but should it happen, everything's bad. My gram said it's the creole in me that gives me that extra spice of attitude and as I leaned my body against the counter I fumed. *Aint that about nothing!*

Lance came over to me and gently nudged my shoulder. He assured me he would get to the bottom of it and make sure the car was back to normal. He suggested we go the grocery store since there was nothing more we could do about it at the moment. I closed my eyes, then grabbed my list and my purse. We needed to get to the store, and I needed to walk off some steam.

The grocery store wasn't as packed as I thought it would be on a late summer morning, which was good because I managed to find a shawl to cover my sling, but anyone who was really looking would see something was

41

wrong the way the material laid down. We maneuvered up and down the aisles with ease. Lance stayed close to me, his holster hidden from anyone nearby. I could see him paying attention to everyone within earshot as we strolled through and I frowned. *He's gonna have to be not so obvious if he has to be by my side like this cause he was really gonna give himself away.*

Lance added items from my list to the cart as I checked things off. Because I normally made enough food for leftovers the next day I figured I could still buy like I usually did, I just wouldn't have anything extra. Walking up towards the cleaning supplies, I grabbed disinfectant spray, air fresheners, gloves, bleach, and anything else I could think of for my car. It pissed me off that they would be so disrespectful like that. That just showed me that these people weren't from around here. As far as I was concerned, those assholes could buy me another car if none of this worked.

With the cart filled about halfway, I figured it would be enough for the both of us for a while. Once in the checkout I grabbed a newspaper to hand to the clerk and reached in my purse to get my money. I turned back just as Lance was folding his wallet up and taking the receipt from the clerk. I didn't argue, especially since my car smelled like old cabbage and cheese. *It's the least the government could do.*

We made our way out to Lance's truck then to the motel that he had been staying at about twenty minutes away so that he could get the rest of his things and check out. I took out the paper I got at the store to read while he was in the office. An article caught my attention immediately.

Police and a Federal agency were called to Surpent Park two days ago. While full details have yet to be released due to the pending investigation, it was reported that a high-speed chase between two cars ended in the park. An eyewitness told the Lane Post that a woman in her late twenties was pursued by a car full of men into the park. The witness also told us that once the police got there the men were taken into custody and the woman was carried out by an officer to the ambulance. The name of the woman and the suspects have not been released at this time.

They went on to talk about Mr. Bates and how his murder was a senseless crime and that the police believed it was connected to the chase that was reported. They praised him as a hero for trying to protect his community from criminals. Services were set to be held in a couple of days and even though I knew what dealings he was in; I was determined to go to pay my respects. I didn't know that side of Mr. Bates and I still didn't want to think of him that way.

I sat holding my breath reading the rest. They pretty much told everything except my name. Lance got back in to the truck and I showed him what I read.

"I'll contact the chief and see what he wants to do," Lance said as we headed back to my place. I bit my nails the whole way, the anger I felt earlier had been placed by nervousness.

♫

The morning of the funeral I found a dark skirt and blouse that covered my stitches and brace. I walked down the stairs and to the kitchen to get some coffee. Lance was at the counter on his laptop and looked up, his eyebrows raised.

"Mr. Bates funeral is today." Lance stood up.

"I don't think that's a good idea." Surprised at his response I put my purse down.

"And just why the hell not?"

"Because of your arm and we still don't..."

"Don't give me that. I'm not gonna wear the sling and the brace on my arm is covered. Y'all gonna be swarmed like bees there anyway, right?" He put his hands up.

"I know you're upset but I gotta make the call here. Now there are people out there that are more than likely looking for you. Being out like that with a crowd makes you a target." I looked at him and huffed. There really could be people out there looking for me. Even so, I wasn't going to not show up, I had to pay my respects.

"All I'm saying is..."

"You say what you want, I'm going. Besides, if I don't at least show up, people will wonder why. This is a small town, something like this and you're not there, people will talk."

Lance picked up the phone and called it in to tell them what the plan was. He told me to wait so he could

44

change his clothes and came back down in minutes with black pants and a black shirt. We got into his truck and I directed him to Pine Creek Cemetery which was just on the outskirts of town. I rolled the window down and let the hot air hit me as we drove down there with me mumbling directions under my breath.

We made it to the cemetery late. I could see and hear the pastor in the middle of the eulogy from where we were parked. I put my hand on the door handle but Lance stopped me.

"I can't let you out of the truck to go down there; it's too dangerous. We have tons of resources on deck but this is too open." I stared at him, pissed and biting my lip hard. Lance didn't budge from his stance and I knew this battle was gonna be a loss for me so I turned my head and rolled down the window enough so people could acknowledge I was there if they walked by. I was sure everyone who saw me would buy the fact that I wasn't down there at the plot because it was too much. I wouldn't have been surprised if most people were doing the same as me. This rocked the town to its core, we just didn't have anything like this happen here.

About fifty people came out and as I looked around at familiar faces, my eyes rested on the coffin and a sadness came over me. Poor Mr. Bates, he was always a nice man and everybody enjoyed him. Tears brimmed my eyelids and I wiped them away.

I went from seeing Mr. Bates smiling to seeing him lying on the ground covered in blood. I could have done something, anything. Instead, I was a coward, I just left him there alone. I felt like a horrible person at that moment, watching the scene play in my head. Tears flowed freely down my cheeks and I cried to myself. No matter how hard I tried, I just couldn't get the image of his body out of my head. When I looked back at the cemetery, everything was blurry, but I could see the crowd starting to disperse. Tissue came into my view as Lance leaned over and gave it to me.

"Thank you," I said sniffing and wiping my eyes. I turned and looked back at the thinning crowd that was heading our way.

"We should get out of here," Lance said and started the truck to head back to my house. The closer we got to my side of town, the sadder I got. Not being too far away from the general store, I made him stop by. I felt the need to see it again. We pulled up to the curb and I looked out through the window staring at the place I went to at least once a month. Yellow caution tape was hanging from the front of the entrance and there was a closed sign hanging up in the window. It was gloomy and dark even though the sun was shining brightly.

Unbelievable, just unbelievable. If you would have asked me five years ago where I would be now, I never would have told you this. I know the saying goes 'everything happens for a reason', but this makes no sense what so ever. I wanted someone to explain to me what was happening and why. We stayed a moment longer then went back to my house.

Depressed, I trudged up the short path and opened the door. Walking straight into my spare room where Gram's piano was, I sat down on the bench. I tapped the keys and thought about her. I just knew she would be able to answer my questions, but she wasn't here. Though she had been gone for years, I felt like I could feel her when I was in this room. Gram used to spend hours playing hymns while I sat next to her with my favorite doll. We talked about everything under the moon and sun and she always knew what to say. Gram had that 'ole soul' as her friends called it. She looked like the grandmas on the movies, you know with the short round body and silvery hair that was perfectly rolled tight. Her accent was so strong that those who didn't know her couldn't quite understand her mumble, but I did.

"Chile, you gots butta fingas." I would look at my hands and back to her.

"I ain't got butter on my fingers Gram." She would pat me with her chubby hands.

"Yes, you do. Them fingas glaze over them ivories like butta… smooth."

I smiled and went over the keys again. I tried to lift my left arm to play but it was too stiff so I settled for a soft medley that I could do on one hand and imagined her next to me. I could hear Gram humming softly and it brought a smile to my lips. I played for a while and began to relax as time passed. Taking a deep breath, I closed the top and got up. Lance was standing in the doorway; I didn't even know he had been there. My mood went from chill to irritation because I just wanted some time alone. I stormed by and went to my room slamming the door. I heard his footsteps then the door creaked open and I sat up angry.

"Ok, look now, I need a moment, can I have that please?"

"Leave the door open." I stood up.

"This is my goddamn room, if I want it shut it's going to be shut!"

"Not on my watch." I walked up to him.

"Who the hell do you think you are? This is my house, my room. You just not gonna come in here and start barking orders. Now if I want my door shut, it's gonna be shut!" Lance didn't back down and stood in the doorway not saying a word. I was beyond pissed off.

"Why are you still standing there? I need some space! Nobody is in my house so back off!" Words were coming out of my mouth and I didn't care. I was upset and sad and everything else. My fist was clenched and I felt like throwing something. He had some nerve telling me what to do in my own house.

"I'm trying to do my job so if that means you leave your door open then you need to leave your door open. I'm going to be blunt with you, if you want to shut that door, be my guest, but if I can't get to you fast enough and something happens that is on you. You have no idea what you're in the middle of right now. This is not some movie, this is real life, your life. You can figure out what you want to do." He turned and walked back down the stairs. I was left with my mouth wide open. *Did this fool really just talk like that to me in my house?* I slammed my door back shut.

First, I thought I'll kick his ass out on the sidewalk and he can watch me from there. I sat back on the bed and stared at the door. Then I thought about what he just said to me. Who says something like that? I mean if you want to scare someone, telling them you may not be able to get to them is promising. As much as I hated it, I knew that whatever hell I was in I needed to listen.

I was still mad but I didn't want him to know he won this battle so I got up and slowly opened the door, the creaks seemed louder and louder as it widened. I stared around the room and stomped to my drawer to pull out a change of clothes. I slammed my drawer and went to the bathroom slamming that door. I was acting childish but I didn't care. I carefully changed and came out to sit back on the bed, then I fell back on the mattress, grabbed a pillow and threw it out the door, hearing it fall down the stairs.

W. Owens

Lance

He could feel the anger coming off Maxie as he explained what was going to happen in the next coming days. As with anyone who would be in a situation like this, he could understand. A complete stranger now in your home for an extended amount of time, your privacy is gone and you feel like you have no control of your life at the moment.

Lance wanted to be as professional as he could and try to stay out of her way within reason. He knew that she would need help with some things because of her injury, though he had reason to believe that she would try to be independent. When Lance accepted this assignment of protective duty from his chief he spent the first night researching in the small townhouse since it was the first time in a unique situation like this. He figured if he followed everything on his to-do list there shouldn't be any concerning issues.

First step, be as courteous as possible to Maxie, that included being respectful of her and her things. Second, make her feel safe; Lance wanted Maxie to not be afraid and believe that he would do everything in his power to keep her out of harm's way. Third, make her feel comfortable around him. He wasn't used to being a roommate to anyone, let

51

alone a beautiful woman so Lance was going to have to try and not be a stickler. Fourth, in order for all of this to work, she needed to trust him. So far things were looking a little dim.

Lance was on high alert mode when he heard Maxie yelling from upstairs; what he didn't expect was what he saw when he burst through the door. Maxie in a towel, her long wet curly hair falling off her shoulder, caramel colored legs smooth as silk uncovered. Lance thought she was beautiful when he saw her the first time, but he was speechless in that doorway. Even as she held her arm in pain, she was beautiful. He had to shake the cobwebs out of his head because the reality of it was she was a witness and he was only there to do his job, not ogle her.

He could tell that Mr. Bates meant something to Maxie the way she reacted at the cemetery. She hadn't really had time to take all of it in and thinking she would be ok, she wanted to pay her respects. He should have stopped her but didn't because of that. Loss was something Lance knew all too well and he could admit that no matter how strong you were, it can pull you down on your knees in an instant. He was pretty masculine himself but when it came to a woman crying, it did something to him. Lance could remember when his dad passed away and how devastated his mom was. She'd cried for days and every time he'd been there to comfort her until she could get herself together. She'd needed that, just like Maxie needed someone in her time of grieving, he just wasn't sure how to be there, she was a stranger after all.

52

Maxie

I was still in a funk cloud from the other day when things got heated between the two of us. My attitude hadn't been and still wasn't pleasant. Lance kept his distance but he was still too close for me. When I had to sit with him to discuss things over again about this arrangement, I tried my best to be calm, but I could feel the foul feelings building inside slowly. Lance explained to me how this was going to work for the time being and I wasn't happy. *How do I go from being single and living alone to having a stranger in my house, who basically has to watch my every move within a week?*

"If you do have to go out, you won't go with your sling so we won't draw attention, but we will keep that to a minimum for now anyway."

"What am I supposed to say about you? I told you before this was a small town."

"We'll figure it out when the time comes. But I think we will stick to going to neighboring towns when leaving out."

"I have to let my boss know, cause I'm sure y'all don't want me going to work. What about handling that?" Lance thought for a moment.

"Family emergency, or a much-needed vacation; which would be more believable?" I had to think about that. I had cousins scattered throughout Texas mostly and some in Ohio. My daddy's brother Lee lived on the Air Force base with his family near San Antonio. My parents were in Texarkana and knowing my boss, he would call and check on me in one of those places if it was an emergency.

"Vacation. I've never taken one." Lance nodded and smiled slightly.

"Workaholic I see." I shook my head.

"No, I just love my job is all." He asked what I did for a living and I told him I was a piano player for Land's Down Lounge & Bar.

"What days do you usually work?"

"It depends on the week. I share days with another piano player. This week I'm off until Thursday night."

"You need to call your boss as soon as you can," Lance said, "You can say something like you won a cruise and it has to be used ASAP."

"I wish I could be on a cruise," I mumbled. "Far away from here." Lance ignored my comment.

"We want to play this as normal as possible, with the exception of going to work because that could be an easy target. With that being said, you're right, this is a small town, if people don't see you from time to time they may come looking and attention is what you don't need. Is there anything you normally do extracurricular?"

"There's a local gym I go sometimes, but I normally go to the Flea Market in Houston and a record store once a week."

"What day do you go?" I felt like I was being interrogated because it was like I almost had to tell when I took showers and when I slept and ate too.

"Today. Usually I'm almost out the door by now." Lance nodded.

"Let's get ready to go then."

I wanted to argue but kept my mouth shut because so far I hadn't won any of my protests. Defeated and upset, I climbed my stairs and managed to change into some jogging pants and hoodie. After several minutes of trying to put my hair up, I gave up and settled for it down which didn't help my mood at all. Putting my sling on, I walked downstairs to see Lance waiting for me, looking out of place. His clothes didn't even say 'I'm visiting', he looked as obvious as the sun in the sky on a clear blue day. It was the same type clothes he's been wearing since I've seen him. The attitude moved a little more up my anger pot.

We got in his truck and headed towards Houston, with me guiding him there. Lance tried to make small talk but I was brooding. This used to be my favorite ride once a week, just me and the road and my music. Now I'm sharing my 'me' time. I put my elbow on the edge of the lowered window and stared out into the land that raced past me. Trees and crops were painted beyond the road. *By now, I'd be popping gum and singing to a tune, instead, I'm stuck in the damn passenger seat with him.*

I glanced over at Lance. Dark shirt with a V-neckline, his arms hugged tightly to his muscular arms. Dark cargo pants *again* and hiking boots, yeah he stuck out like a sore thumb in a hot wing contest. The more I looked at him the more I was irritated. I couldn't take it anymore, I was gonna say something.

"What's your deal," I asked him frowning.

"Excuse me?"

"Don't you have other clothes? I've seen you for days and it's always the same stuff, even the mountain boots."

"What's mountain boots?" I pointed to his feet.

"Those huge clunker-looking boots. I mean damn, don't make it obvious you aren't from here." It was Lance's turn to frown. I knew I shouldn't have, but I kept going on.

"That's not gonna work," I said pointing to the clothes. "And that," I said, pointing to the boots, "Ain't gonna work either. You're in the south, nobody dresses like that. Might as well put me in the middle of downtown with bright lights." I kept going and going and I could see him tensing up more and more.

Lance suddenly stopped on the pull off side of the road and put the truck in park. I don't know why I wanted to push his button, but I really wanted to push his button. Must have been all the attitude that spilled out my pot. He got out and walked around to my side of the truck. Opening the back passenger door, he opened a duffel bag and pulled out some tennis shoes. Then pulling out a printed shirt, Lance took what he had on off and switched out. My mouth dropped open.

"Are you serious right now? Right here on the highway?" Not saying a word, Lance got back into the truck and we took off again. Of course, that made me more pissed, making my pot of anger worse.

We pulled up to the flea market and I took my sling off before getting out the truck. I instantly smelled fresh funnel cakes and popcorn, turkey legs and deep-fried goodness. I could feel my stomach growl with excitement. I just loved the flea market, there were so many treasures you could find there. I spent hours just wondering around exploring. Mama and Gram and I used to come on the weekends to stroll the grounds, always coming out with something to put somewhere.

My excitement turned to foulness when I remembered I wasn't alone. Lance rounded the truck and waited for me to lead the way. Huffing, I spun on my heels and almost stomped out the parking lot. *Uggghh why me?!*

Starting up the rows and making our way to a clothing stand, Lance was practically at my ankles. I would feel his breath if he got any closer. By now I was heated, how was I supposed to do anything normal with him acting like a stalker? I could feel another outburst on the edge of my lips. My day was not going well.

"You know," I whispered back to him, "I'd feel better if you walked beside me and not behind me. It looks weird, and why do you have to act all stiff, loosen up. You probably look creepy like that too...damn." He fell into step with me. From the corner of my eye, I could see Lance's lips tighten up.

"Ok, now you're too close, you're smothering me." He stopped off to the side a distance away from the nearest stand I let him have it. All that I had been feeling finally spilled out of my pot and onto the floor.

"I can't do this. I'm trapped and it ain't right. You see what I just did to you? It didn't feel good, did it? You might as well be a Goddamn babysitter! Oh wait, you already are. Telling me what I can and can't do..." I probably sounded like I was three the way I was pouting.

"You're not making this easy and I want it easier.... Shit! Can you do that? Do you know what easy is? It's acting normal, and this ain't normal you breathin down my neck." I'm sure I didn't make my argument any better when I stomped my foot. Lance stood there for a moment looking at me.

"Easier... I can do that." He grabbed my hand into his and pulled me with him.

Oh hell, I thought as we went towards the stands again. We made it to a bracelet stand and Lance stopped in front of some handmade bracelets.

"Sweetheart look. This one has astrological signs on it. Isn't yours Taurus?" He picked it up examined the small trinkets around the band.

"Yeah, I think this is yours because you're as mean as a bull." My face felt hot and I could see Lance looking at the vendor, a smirk playing on his face.

"Soft and calm, but a beast on the outside when you least expect it. This one right here, don't make her mad." Lance and the dealer took a crackle of laughs out on me as he told more jokes.

"How much?" Lance asked going to his back pocket.

"No, I'm good. I don't need it," I mumbled, embarrassed down to my toes. I wasn't ready for that at all. The dealer looked at Lance then to me and said, "It's one of a kind, let your honey get it for you, sounds like it fits you right."

"I think it's too big for my wrist. Thank you though." I pulled Lance away, once again we were in a small area. I stood there for a moment looking at him. It was obvious what I was dishing out could be sent right back with no problem. *Looks like I wasted my time with the attitude.* I sighed defeat.

"Ok, Ok. I'm done. Can we just stop?"

"That's up to you," he replied. I took a deep breath and sighed.

"Look, I've been frustrated about all of this. How would you feel if things changed and you felt like you had no control of anything?" I held my sore wrist with my other hand.

"I know you're doing your job, this just sucks right now." Lance looked at me, his hardened face softening.

"That's all I'm trying to do, my job. I know this isn't easy for you, It's not easy for me either, but you have to try and understand this is serious and no one wants anything to happen to you." He looked away for a moment then back to me.

"Look, you cut me some slack and I'll relax just a little. I can't completely back down because that defeats the purpose of me being here in the first place, but I'll work on it, deal?" He held out his hand and I reluctantly took it.

"And you are right," he said. "I do need to loosen up and act more natural. Let's say we both do that?" I nodded in agreement. What was the point of me making it difficult if he wasn't going to go anywhere anyway? We stared at each other in truce, the anger was slowly going away. I could see him begin to take notice of all the stands in detail.

"I've never been to a flea market before," Lance revealed to me as he kept my hand clasped in his and we started making our way down the main strip. Even though it was odd he didn't let go, I didn't object. Normal, right?

"There's nothing to it, you basically just walk and stop. I hope those shoes are comfortable." I could feel him relax, but only a bit, he was still taking notice of the surroundings and taking in people who walked past. I was thinking maybe the rest of the trip would be halfway decent now as I led him to a hat stand.

♫

Almost two hours and lots of footwork later, I was just about done with my trip. My pain was getting bothersome and I was surprisingly tired. Lance seemed to have enjoyed looking at all the things the market had and ended up buying jade and turquoise stones which were the prettiest shades of greens and blues I had ever seen. I managed to find another two trinkets to add to my cabinet at home. One was a baby angel about three inches tall made out of glass. You could see all the delicate features on it and if you held it to the light, it sparkled rainbow colors. The other trinket was a porcelain fairy, which I was immediately drawn to. She was in a praying position looking up, a single tear was painted on her face.

Sadness came over me as I turned it in my hand, thinking of Mr. Bates, his lovely fairy is what he called me all the time. I shook that out of my head as soon I felt myself choke up a little. I didn't feel like crying today. Looking at my watch, I told Lance we should probably start for the record store before they closed for the day.

At my favorite food stand I bought deep-fried pickles before we headed to the truck. The twenty-minute drive would consist of me stuffing my face the whole way. I put my sling on and took a couple of ibuprofen.

"You drive out here once a week?" Lance asked as he pulled onto the highway.

"Yep," I said popping the fried pickle in my mouth. Lance looked over at the food in my lap and turned his face up.

"Hey now, don't fly by it unless you try it, here." Hesitantly, he took it as I popped another in my mouth. I looked out the window. *3, 2, 1...*

"Can I have another one?" I smiled and handed him two more. *Never fails.*

I ate the rest before we made it to the record store parking lot. I took the sling off and tried to straighten my arm out, it was pretty stiff and my wrist was getting tight around the brace. I was gonna have to make this visit quick.

When we entered I forgot all about the pain, I was in heaven. This was my favorite place to go, there were thousands and thousands of vinyl just sitting around waiting to be picked up and played. I was never looking for anything, but I always came out with something. Vin, the store owner came through every visit with a treasure. He was always sure he would have something I would like, and I was never disappointed.

"Look what ole Vin found for you," Vin Lex said as he rounded the corner of a long counter. He was your typical Jersey boy who was a transplant fifteen years ago with slick back black hair, sunglasses sitting on top, a gold chain, and tightly fitted shirt that showed all his oversized muscles. All the local talent visited Vin because even when you thought you couldn't find something, Vin had it.

"Oh my God, you left the label blank. You know I love surprises, you're my hero Jersey." I took the record and kissed him on the cheek. I told him I was going to look around a bit longer and be ready shortly. Lance actually stepped away and found interest in something flipping a record to the back cover. The bin he was at had a label listing 1972 on it. I flipped through a couple more vinyls then walked over to him.

"You can't beat the classics, that's a good bin right there." He nodded in agreement. I went to the counter and only got the one record with him trailing behind. Vin told me he would see me next week. I looked at Lance then back at Vin.

"I'm going on a much-needed vacation Jersey. When I get back I'm sure I'll have a list by then." He looked over at Lance then back at me.

"You must be someone special if you get the pleasure of spending a vacation with my girl here. You never told me you were taken beautiful." Vin's heart is broken; the world has ended." I didn't say a word because I didn't want to start lying out my ass. Instead, I laughed and headed out the store grabbing Lance's hand along the way. It was time to get back to the reality of home.

At some point on the way back, I dozed off. When I woke up, it looked late as we pulled up to my place. I was so sore I winced all the way to the door, tears brimming my eyes. I knew I did too much today, but I wasn't thinking. Lance was nice enough to help me in and get me settled with ice and medicine. After a light dinner, I decided to call it a night because it had been a long day. Lying down, I thought about the past couple of days. Everything felt like a blur, and I couldn't get a clear picture of any of it. Eventually, my eyes closed, but my mind was still spinning.

I was at Bate's General Store standing next to Mr. Bates at the cash register. Some guys came in and started to argue with him. Next thing I knew, I could hear him saying, "Run lovely fairy, run!" I was frozen, my legs couldn't move. I heard the gun go off.

My eyes flew open and I sat up. I was in my bed, in my room. Looking around, the only light was coming from the glow of the alarm clock: 2:35am. I stayed sitting for a moment glancing around, then got up and put my robe on. Shaking the visions out, I made it downstairs to get water. The dull light from the oven top cast shadows everywhere. Trying not to wake Lance up, I crept down the last steps and quietly rounded the couch. I could see him on his back with arms crossed and one leg up, eyes closed. I almost made it to the short hallway.

"It wouldn't matter how quiet you are; I'd still hear you." I threw my hand up, turned around, and put it on my hip.

"Do you sleep?"

"Yeah."

"When? Cause I've never seen you do it."

"Well, I do. I should be asking you that question." He sat up and looked at me. I had no clue what he was talking about.

"Excuse me?"

"I've heard you tossing and turning every night since I've been here, but tonight you were all over the place." I knew I had been really tired in the mornings but I couldn't figure out why; sounds like I had my answer.

"Really?" I asked. Lance nodded. I turned to walk to the kitchen and he followed me.

"Bad dream?" I looked at him, I wasn't sure I wanted to tell him because he was still a stranger to me but at the same time, I didn't have anyone else to talk to at the moment. I grabbed water sat at the stool and nodded.

"Do you want to talk about it?" I shook my head no. That was something I didn't want to think about again, and if it went to the back of my mind, I was fine with it. There was just something unsettling about it that kept me from going there. Lance leaned back on the counter and was quiet. I fiddled with the cap on the bottle. Crickets chirped outside the window and I stared out in that direction. He sounded sincere in asking me if I wanted to talk about my dream. I'm not sure why but I suddenly felt bad for how I had been acting towards him and right now, he was trying to be nice. It was like just then I realized he wasn't the enemy; he was the good guy.

"Sorry for showing my ass lately. I promise I don't act like that all the time." Lance moved from where he was and took a step towards me.

"I'm sure I fit that profile earlier myself." He leaned his hand on the counter and came a little closer.

"I'm actually a Taurus myself." And just like that, he walked back in the living room and I sat there smiling softly. I had to admit that was a pretty good comeback Lance had at the market, especially with the way I had been acting, that was definitely deserving. I sat there a moment longer then took my water bottle and headed upstairs.

"Like the slippers by the way," Lance said from the couch. I looked down at my musical notes that covered my feet and smiled again.

Lance

He wanted to tell her to try and bear with everything, but he also wanted her to know how serious the situation was, he just didn't want to scare her.

Maxie had Lance a little frustrated. For someone as pretty as she was, he thought she had been acting ugly. It really started the morning of the funeral then it built up from there. He knew where her anger was coming from but she wasn't giving him any type of break. And when it came to him giving a direction, she wasn't having it.

Lance let his frustration flush when she snapped at him regarding her privacy but he wanted her to understand that this was real, all of it, and if she didn't let things go as they needed to, something could happen to her. He knew it was all emotion, but for some reason, she got the best of him. Lance usually kept his composure even in intense situations. He couldn't figure out why or how Maxie hit the right button, but she did and he slipped. Be that as it may, when she opened her bedroom sometime later, he knew she took what he was saying as truth.

He could see the look of shock on her face when he pulled off the highway and changed his shirt and shoes.

Lance thought his actions were what caused her to fuss even more, but at that point, he didn't care. If she was trying to upset him, it was finally working, especially when he called her out at the market. He knew that was unprofessional, but he had enough of the jabs and he thought he had been doing a pretty good job with his task.

Lance was beginning to think this was going to be a long couple of weeks being around her. He was hoping at least that it was going to get a little better. Arguing with a woman every day was not his ideal assignment by any means, so when they made the rest of the day and night without incident, hope was glimmering in the back of his mind.

Maxie

I called my boss Tyler at the lounge and told him I needed to talk with him asap. I decided to stick with the story of going on a vacation and needing to leave right away. I made sure I wasn't wearing my sling but put a poncho sweater on to hide the wrist brace. My job was within walking distance from my house, but Lance insisted he drive me over there.

Coming through the door, I immediately looked up to the piano at the stage and sadness overcame me. I so wanted to go up there and play, but I knew I couldn't. Walking past the bar and patron tables, we headed to the back to Tyler's office. Pictures were hanging with famous singers all over the walls. The desk was covered with papers and a huge jelly bean container. Tyler Johnson's vice was jelly beans; you couldn't see jelly beans without seeing Tyler.

He greeted us at the door, looking at Lance first, then back to me. I introduced everyone around with Lance being a friend of mine. Tyler was a short middle aged man with coffee colored skin and the most beautiful hazel eyes you have ever seen. He wore his hair in a short afro and still wore Brut cologne. He was a pretty cool guy, always making sure his staff and customers were taken care of. I didn't want to screw him over by not being here, but at the same time, I knew there would be no way of this coming out good if I continued to work while people were possibly looking for me. I came up with a story that I thought would be believable for everyone, but not crazy. We sat down at the desk and Tyler immediately grabbed a handful of jelly beans.

"What's going on my love?"

"You know how I always enter in contests for vacations and money and all that? Well, I finally won." I grinned from ear to ear.

"You did? Oh, man, looks like I need to start doing that too," Tyler said congratulating me. I looked over at the mountain of candy on the desk.

"So here's the catch. The trip needs to be taken ASAP, as in I need to go in the next couple of days." Tyler stopped smiling and looked at me questioningly.

"I see that look, Tyler. Get Jerry, he's as good as me," I said to him and he chuckled. "You're giving Jerry too much credit." He leaned back in the chair and looked at both of us.

"I don't want to ask but I know I need to, how long is the trip?" I looked at Lance then back at Tyler, a nervous look on my face.

"Two weeks." Tyler's eyes bugged out of his head.

"Two weeks? Maxie, you're killing me."

"You know I deserve this Tyler. I've never had a real vacation. I promise when I get back I'll work every day for a month if you need me to." Lance folded his hands. After a couple minutes of protesting, Tyler looked at the both of us and finally agreed to my time off. I gave him a huge hug and told him I needed to get going to pack. Before we made it to Lance's truck, Tyler came out after us.

"If they have those sweet beans where you're going, bring me back some hon." I smiled and gave him a wink.

"You know I will."

♫

"One of the men in custody gave some useful information. He told us about the shipments that run here in Texas and also told us the names of people that handle this area. There are twelve men… we have eight of them. This also includes a couple of men in the photos I showed you before."

"That's great. How soon do you think you will have the other men?" We were sitting in my living room and Lance just got off the phone with FGA with an update. It had been a couple days and he hadn't had any word on anything.

"It's not that simple," Lance replied. "We may have some leads, but this is just here in Texas, we are still not as close as you think. These guys have been in illegal dealings for a long time, it's not gonna go away overnight." There was a pause, "I would like to put you in Witness Protection until I feel comfortable."

I sighed and looked around my home. Everything familiar was here, my pictures, my clothes, my bedroom and my piano. Needless to say, I wasn't the most excited person in the world to be told I have to leave and go a strange place. I didn't like the idea and it showed on my face. Lance saw my expression and reached to take my hand.

"I know this is hard, but I want you to know this is to ensure…"

There was a crash at my kitchen sliding door, I jumped up and could see two men bursting in. I ran up my stairs screaming as Lance charged and tackled one of them. Reaching the top, I was tripped up by a hand to my ankle. I fell on my side, pain shooting in all directions. Kicking the man, I scrambled up and grabbed the first thing in sight, a statue that was leaning on the floor. I turned and swung as the man lunged towards me, connecting with his face and sending him backwards down the stairs, blood spurting in all directions as he fell.

With him motionless, I ran back down and towards the front door just as Lance was knocked up against the wall. The man pulled a gun out of his pocket and turned towards me. I could see Lance pull out his gun and fire twice. I ducked and fell to the floor covering myself as I heard more shots. I could hear footsteps coming closer. Hands grabbed and gently lifted me up on my feet, it was Lance. I could see the man on the ground behind him, he looked dead.

"Oh my God!" I shrieked.

"We have to leave now," Lance said urgently. I looked back at the man at the bottom of the stairs, who still hadn't moved. Lance grabbed his laptop and we ran out the door to his truck. The tires squealed as we peeled down the street and headed for the expressway. My heart was beating out of my chest, tears still streaking down my face and I was holding my wrist. Lance grabbed his cellphone.

"There's been a compromise at Maxie McHill's location, we are going dark. I'll contact you when we are clear." Lance hung up the phone and threw it out the window. He turned and looked over at me.

"Don't worry, you will be safe soon. I'll make sure of it."

I stared out of the truck window as we worked down the road. I had no idea where we were going but I knew wherever it was I wanted to be far away. I didn't want to speak, I just stared out in a daze. It seemed as though my life turned completely upside down in a short matter of time and now people were trying to kill me. I always thought in the back of my mind it could happen, but to actually know without a doubt was terrifying.

When I fell at my house on the stairs, I had used my bad arm to try and catch myself. It was throbbing and my hip felt bruised up. I don't even remember hitting it on anything, but I must have because it hurt bad. I didn't want to say anything about it because that was one more thing Lance would have to worry about. He saw me some time after we had been on the road for a while cringing and grabbing myself when he hit a bump.

Lance eventually pulled over at the first gas station he saw and grabbed a duffel bag in the back. Getting out a first aid kit, he quickly got a bottle and one of those ice packs you snap in the bag and makes it cold. He gently placed it on my arm gave me two pills to help with the pain. We were back on the road in less than two minutes.

More time passed as we rode on which meant that more time passed for me to fully understand what was going on. The reality of knowing that I could have been killed for a second time didn't go over well and my eyes were swollen from the tears I shed almost the whole time. As hard as I tried, I couldn't keep it together. I wanted to make myself as hard as possible and wish it all away but nothing helped.

I didn't like for anyone to see me vulnerable but this was all too much. Every now and then, I would look out the window to hide my face so Lance wouldn't see me even though I knew that he could. I trembled until he reached in the back and grabbed a jacket, placing it on me while he paid attention to the road.

"You're going to be ok, I promise," he kept telling me. The last thing I told him before dozing off was, "Please don't break that promise."

♫

I awoke to the sound of birds chirping and bright sunlight behind my eyelids. Looking around, I noticed I was in a bed surrounded by beautiful Earth tone walls and a cozy décor. Lance was in a chair to the left of me.

"Good Morning." Sitting up and blinking rapidly, I looked around again. *Where in the world am I?*

"I don't remember walking in here," I said looking around and rubbing my eyes to clear them up.

"You didn't. I carried you in here."

"Seriously?"

"Yeah." He sat up straighter and looked at my arm.

"Your bandage needs to be changed." I looked down and could see blood had seeped through my shirt. Lance got up from the chair and walked out the room. He returned with a towel, bandages, and clothes.

"You can shower and try this on. If you need help with the bandages let me know." Puzzled, I took the clothes and looked at him. He stared back at me.

"I'll explain everything after you come back." I slowly got up from the bed, took a step and winced. My hip hurt bad; Lance was immediately by my side. I put my weight mostly on him and was helped into the bathroom. As Lance was turning on the shower, I was looking at myself in the mirror. I looked like a bum, my shirt was stained with blood, my hair was all over the place, even the brace looked messed up. Tears welled up in my eyes and I turned away.

"Let me help you," Lance said softly. I looked up at him blurry eyed. I felt helpless and dazed; like this was all a bad, bad dream and I couldn't wake up. Taking me over to the edge of the tub he sat me down. Very slowly, he took off my wrist brace and had me lift my arms up as he pulled off my shirt. Lance looked at the bandage then ran his hand under the water from the shower. Making it wet, he was able to peel the whole thing off. Red blotches were around the stitches.

"I'll be right outside this door." He turned and closed the door behind him. I sat there, my mind still swirling. I didn't know where I was but for some reason, I didn't have the fear like I did when I was nearly attacked. Undressing, I saw a bruise the size of an orange had formed on my hip and that made me choke back as steam enveloped me. Painfully I entered the shower, letting the warm water course down my body, trying to drain my tears away.

Luckily, the sundress allowed me to climb into it so that I didn't have to pull it over my head. Unfortunately, there was a zipper in the back. I knew I was going to need some help with the dress and the bandage. I stepped out of the bathroom and back into the bedroom. Lance had already showered and changed into tan cargo pants and a white shirt. He looked different than earlier, refreshed even. I limped over with the bandages and brace in my hand.

"I need help with this, but I need help with something else."

"Ok," he said.

"This dress has a zipper in the back and I can't get it up, can you help me?" I turned around so he could zip up the dress. Afterwards, I tried to sit on the edge of a chair while he checked the stitches and cleaned the area with antiseptic. I grimaced in pain. "Relax," he said gently. I took a deep breath and sighed.

"Well, the good news is, everything looks fine, even though there was a lot of blood on your arm. I would say another couple of days and the stitches can come out." Lance tried to offer me an icepack but I waved him off. I was barely listening because I was busy looking around.

"Where are we?" I asked. He looked at me then tended back to my arm.

"We are somewhere where no one can find you." I stared at him.

"It's not an FGA safe house," Lance said.

"Why not, isn't that where you said I needed to go?" He stood up.

"I really don't think you need a bandage anymore." I looked down at my arm. It wasn't as bad as it first looked before the shower.

"So, I'm not at a safe house, but no one can find me?"

"Yes."

I looked directly at him, confusion surfacing.

"What's going on Lance?" He sat down next to me again, wearing a serious expression.

"The men who came to your house were part of Meek. I recognized their faces from photos I reviewed before. It's out about you and Mr. Bates murder." Lance rubbed his goatee.

"Rather than take you to a safe house, I thought it would be best to go off the path without FGA knowing the exact location of our whereabouts for now. I haven't figured out how news got out because only key people knew. Everything has been classified and I would hate to think there is a mole within FGA." He looked at me and I started looking around the big room again.

"McClellanville, South Carolina to answer your first question."

"South Carolina?"

"I want to make sure you are out of sight for now until I can figure things out." I blew out the air I had been holding in the past couple of minutes. Looking around then back at him I asked, "So you're sure no one knows about this place, I'll be ok?"

"No one knows at all, not even FGA, this is my place." Still confused, I sat listening to Lance as he explained how he started renting this cottage about six years ago from an elderly couple who used it as a vacation spot in the winter. They only knew him by his alias, Mr. Roberts. He only used it when he came off long assignments, but as they got older their health began to decline. The couple decided rather than find a stranger to buy their property, offer it to Lance.

"I've had it ever since." I couldn't hear any cars or people or anything except birds. It made me think that maybe we were far from a road. It was almost a little too quiet, I didn't feel like anyone but us existed. I kept thinking I should hear other people until I realized that we weren't at the safe house. *So, did that mean he was gonna leave me here alone?* I had to ask the question that had been at the back of my mind.

"So when do you leave to get back to things?" He shook his head.

"I'm not leaving. I can keep you out of harm's way and the best way is for both of us to stay under the radar. Because of the current situation, the case now goes to the chief officer. My priority is still you; I have everything I need here to stay in the loop."

I was so relieved to know that I wouldn't be alone and even more relieved to know that I would be protected by Lance, who had already proven more than once that he could keep me safe. My mind went to the two men who came for me.

"What happened to the guys at my house?" I asked. Lance rubbed the stubble on his face. He looked a little uncertain about what he was going to tell me.

"You gave one of them a good concussion and a broken nose."

"Good, serves his ass right."

"The other man…." His voice trailed off.

I knew as soon as he stopped talking why he didn't want to tell me, he was dead. Lance killed a man to save me. All this madness around me, and I just wanted it all to stop.

"Now what happens?" I asked rubbing my temple.

"There will be an arraignment for the people we have arrested. If they plead not guilty, a trial date will be set and you will testify on behalf of the state. Because you were a witness to a murder, that will be all they need you for. Once we release all of our evidence, I don't see how we won't get convictions and possibly other members. If they plead guilty then we have to get the all clear that everything is ok for you to go back home. Either way, it will take some time."

"Do you think they will plead not guilty?"

"I think it's unlikely, but you never know. There is enough evidence to bury them for years, and with your testimony that would put the nail in the coffin for them." I wanted to ask what he meant by it will take some time, but changed my mind. Me knowing that wouldn't help in my emotional state, so I stuck with what I knew, which wasn't much.

"But I really didn't see anything," I replied.

"You may think that, but you saw a lot. Between the evidence collected and your eye-witness account, it's a pretty big deal." It sounded like the small town of mine was going to get some attention soon, where everyone knows everybody. It would only be a matter of time once I got back that people will find out what happened to me. My hope was that everything would go as fast as possible.

"When is the arraignment?"

"That really depends on the judge. I'm not familiar with your jurisdiction, so it could take a week or two maybe more. We just have to hold tight until then." I had another question enter my mind as Lance was telling me everything.

Do I need to stay worried?

W. Owens

Lance

When Lance made it to the cottage, Maxie was sound asleep. He didn't want to disturb her as she needed the rest. He opened the passenger door, unbuckled the seatbelt and carefully picked her up. Maxie buried herself in his arms as he headed to the cottage. Opening the front door, he took her directly to the bedroom. After laying her on the bed, he walked through the place, checking every door, window, and room. Lance checked the surveillance screens from the cameras he had throughout the property. He returned to the bedroom and sat down in one of the oversized chairs.

Lance rubbed his eyes; he was exhausted. The long drive south had been almost non-stop from the time they fled Maxie's in the early afternoon to arriving at first light to the house. She stayed quiet pretty much the whole way. He could understand it being an emotional time; one minute you're in your home, the next, running for your life.

The medicine he got from his bag did her well as she fell into a deep sleep which was good considering they had been followed for two hours. Maxie had no clue and he wanted to keep it that way. Not long after they had gotten on the highway Lance noticed a white Cadillac that seemed out of place as it weaved in and out of traffic. He went around a couple of cars and could see it straddle the lane line as if they were trying to keep eye of where the two were going.

Because Lance didn't want Maxie more distressed than she already was, he tried to be as discreet as possible, but when he saw her in pain, he knew he needed to stop and tend to her. Lance calculated the distance the car would close in when he stopped, but also knew that with evening traffic, that they could put more space between them until they reached the outskirts of Texas. He was able to lose the tail enough that he could pull off to the side of the road and take cover in the bushes.

When the car eventually pulled up behind theirs, Lance pulled out his Maxim Nine pistol with silencer and aimed. Blowing out two tires, he waited for them to get out of their car. Guns drawn, Lance didn't give them a chance to look around as he shot them both in the legs. He jumped out of his hiding spot and opening their trunk, threw them both in but not before knocking them out with the butt of his gun. Walking to their car, he noticed a CB radio which he ripped from the dash and threw out the car. Lance grabbed anything of importance and put it in his trunk. He got back behind the wheel and looked over at Maxie, who was still asleep, and continued down the road.

As Lance watched her for some time in the bed, his mind was reeling. He had to figure out how Meek found her. All the precautions were taken to ensure her information was undisclosed, it just didn't make any sense. When Lance finally dozed off, he was still thinking about the men who came after them at the house. Something about it made him feel a little unsettled.

W. Owens

Maxie

After talking for a while, Lance suggested I relax for a bit and then explore inside the cottage while he made something for us to eat.

I closed my eyes after a long time of staring at the ceiling but was too restless so after a few hours of trying to get comfortable, I gave up and decided to get up and to look around. Just outside the bedroom on the second floor, a bathroom stood. To the right, there was a smaller room with electronic equipment and a desk with folders and papers stacked neatly. To the left held a short hallway that led to stairs and opened to a cozy sitting room.

There was a long couch, an oversized chair, an ottoman, and a coffee table. The far wall held a large TV and underneath was a marble mantle that sat a sound stereo system. A hallway by the front door went towards the laundry room and on the left had a small room next to the garage that held exercise equipment.

Through the sitting room was a large spacious kitchen. All of the appliances were up to date and black, the cabinets and drawers were cherry wood and all stood along the length of the wall. Lance was cutting vegetables at the long counter in the middle of the kitchen. The other side of the counter three stools with tall swivel backs stood. He looked up when I entered and smiled. I smiled back lightly and walked to look out the huge bay windows overlooking the backyard.

Next to me stood French doors that opened to a back covered porch. On the other side of the doors was another huge bay window that was opened about halfway. I hesitantly stepped closer and a warm breeze hit my face. Leaning forward I looked out. There was a cobblestone walkway from the porch to the end of the yard. Deep, dark green grass was on either side of the walkway. A large wrought-ironed gate and fence encased the yard about ten yards out and around.

There were two crab apple trees that were on either side of the gate at the back of the yard. From where I could see they were in bloom because the sun was starting to set behind the branches, which enhanced the deep magenta color of the budding flowers. Dark orange rays were streaming into the grass through the shadows. I closed my eyes listening to the sounds from the wind.

I didn't realize Lance was next to me until I heard my name being called; I jumped in surprise and he apologized immediately for scaring me.

"It's ok, I was just looking at everything and zoned out. It's beautiful here," I said looking back into the yard.

"Yes it really is, that's why I like coming here." He opened the French door. "Would you like to go out?" A chill ran through my body, and panic began to set in. I thought back to those men coming through my door at home. I didn't want anyone seeing me, even if we were far away from the nearest neighbor.

"No, that's ok," I said.

Lance nodded understandingly. He shut the door back.

"Ok… Maybe another time then," he said. He looked towards the kitchen. "I've got some food made up, I'm sure you must be hungry." I glanced through the window one more time before turning and following Lance to the table.

Not having much of an appetite, I nibbled on some bread and ate a little of the salad on my plate. Lance talked mostly about the previous owners of the property. I was grateful he was doing most of the talking because inside I was slowly beginning to feel overwhelmed with everything.

The elderly couple had a granddaughter that would come and visit often when they stayed for the season. After she left for college, they decided to leave all her things in case she ever came back to visit. She ended up getting married and moved to Maine, but they left her stuff here, which explained how I had a change of clothes. Lance said they had people upgrade the property before he started renting it from them and after he bought it, there really wasn't too much to do.

Soon, I gave up trying to eat, I decided to go back to the room and look through the closet at the clothes left behind. I could see half the closet were ladies' clothes and the other half was all Lance's. I thought to myself he actually does have real people clothes. Everything looked to be close to my size which was a bonus and one less trip Lance would have to make into town.

"I'm pretty sure that wouldn't be suspicious at all- buying women's clothes alone. Then again you could say they were for you." I remarked as Lance shut the closet door back and turned a smile on his face that revealed deep dimples on either side. "I don't think they would buy that." Smiling lightly back at him I replied, "That is very true."

He checked my arm one more time then wrapped it up for me for the night. I thanked him again for everything.

"If you need me I'll be right in the office, ok?"

"Ok."

Lance left the room and I turned and sat on the bed. I stared out the window for a long time, thinking about everything again. I still felt like I was in a dream and just needed to come to, until I looked at my wrist and pressed down on it, feeling a dull ache. I sighed and laid across the bed, my eyes wide open, and listened to the crickets singing outside until my eyes shut on their own.

I woke up in a ball of knotted sheets, clawing the air. Catching my breath, I looked around the dark room. After a few moments, I realized where I was and put my head back on the pillow. No matter how hard I tried to doze back off again, I couldn't. Trying to take deep breaths, I kept telling myself I was fine. I closed my eyes and the next thing I knew, there was a shadow of a man with his arm raised. I saw the gun drawn right at my head, the barrel staring me down. I was pleading with him to let me go and I wouldn't tell; the gun went off. Heart pounding, I sat on the bed, pulled my knees to my chest and wept. It just wouldn't leave my head. I was alone, in a dark room that wasn't home, and scared. The more I thought about it all, the more I cried. By the time Lance rushed into the room, I was in hysterics.

"It's ok, it's ok." His strong arms sat me up more. I looked at him with swollen eyes, then I buried my face in his chest. "They're gonna find me!" He rubbed my back letting the tears fall on him, promising me they wouldn't. I eventually stopped and wiped my eyes.

"I'm sorry," I sniffed. "I'm just a mess, my mind is all over the place. I'm just going to stay up for a while, sleeping doesn't sound good right now."

"Maxie, you don't need to apologize. You have had a tough couple of days, you're not a mess. But you do need to rest." Lance was quiet for a moment before he spoke again.

"If I stayed in here with you tonight, do you think that would help ease your mind?" I looked around the shadowy room and shivered. I definitely didn't want to be alone in here. I could feel my body getting nervous already. I nodded.

"Ok. I'll be right back?"

He got up and left the room and returned with a thick fleece blanket, two pillows and a box of tissue. He placed them at the foot of the bed and came back to sit next to me with tissue in his hand. I looked down at the floor suddenly embarrassed.

"I'm sorry about this. You aren't getting too tired of me already are you?" He looked at me warmly and handed over some tissue.

"With such a beautiful face, never." I smiled lightly and wiped my eyes.

We sat in silence for a while before I decided to ease back on the pillow. I was suddenly exhausted. Turning to my side and sniffling, Lance put a pillow under my sore arm and wrist then placed a hand on my back. I stared at the dark window for a long time. All this time we had been together prior to getting here, I never thought about all the good things Lance has done for me until now. Besides our hiccup in the beginning, for which I blame myself, he's been very nice. Even now, well I should say, especially now.

"Thanks for keeping me company tonight," I said as I felt more relaxed with each movement of his hand. Lance looked down at me and smiled. "You are very welcome."

Knowing Lance was in there with me set my mind at ease. My eyes lowered soon after and the rest of the night was dreamless. I didn't wake up until the morning, and he was still in the room watching over me.

Lance

Lance felt he had made the right decision bringing Maxie to his cottage. They were so far away at this point no one would ever think to travel to South Carolina, even if they figured out they left the state. Lance and Maxie were still in Texas when Lance stopped their pursuers. He was pretty sure they hadn't been seen because there hadn't been any chatter heard. This place was well secluded from everything, so the chances of being found were slim.

As the evening fell, Lance kept careful watch of Maxie. He could tell she was finally grasping everything that was happening around her. Though she was trying to be strong, he knew it was only a matter of time before it hit her. Those who haven't been in traumatic instances don't know how they will handle it until it happens. When Lance heard her from the other room, he wasn't surprised of the nightmare as much as he was surprised of his immediate urge to comfort her when he saw her on the bed crying. Seeing Maxie so vulnerable tugged at Lance and he didn't know why, but he knew he wanted to make sure she was going be ok, even if that meant that he stayed with her through the night.

W. Owens

Maxie

It had been a few days since we fled to South Carolina. I had started to feel just a little bit better until Lance told me what had been going on back home. Agents had been watching my house in case any more unwanted visitors tried to stop by. There was a mysterious car that parked at the end of the block for two days and no one in the neighborhood made claim to it. Just as strangely as it appeared, it disappeared during a shift change. By the time FGA realized it, they tried to put a tail on the car, but lost it in traffic when it jumped a median and entered an abandoned junkyard. The car was found, but of course, no one was inside. They searched the area for hours and came up with nothing.

Anxiety kicked in and I was a nervous wreck. The thought of Meek watching my house and FGA not being able to find them had my mind going crazy. *How much did they know about me? Are they asking around? They have to know my name because that's how they found my house, right? Wait, what about Mama and Daddy?*

The nightmares came back bad so Lance stayed with me for a couple of days and that was the only way I was able to sleep. As much as I wanted him to stay longer, I felt bad

95

for him sleeping on the floor every night and told him I would be ok if he went back to the office, which is where he had been sleeping. That first night back alone I tossed and turned for an hour, visions swirling in my head. Giving sleep up, I spent my time sitting in a rocker by the window in the room, looking out at the night sky. I was thinking about home, my friends, my job, my house, and everything that meant something to me miles away. I wanted to go home, I wanted things to go back to normal. With tears building up in my eyes, it seemed like that's all I had been doing since coming here; cry, cry, cry, and I'm not a crybaby, but I guess when you have people trying to kill you, emotions take over.

A soft knock on the open door brought me back to the present and I turned to see Lance standing there, in a muscle shirt and sweatpants.

"I didn't believe you when you said you would be ok tonight." He walked over and sat down on the chaise along the window with me. I could see his strong build in the shadow of the moonlight. His size fit him well, not too big like a body-builder, but not too small either. It looked good on him. I realized I had been staring and hoped he didn't notice so I blinked and shook my head.

"Yeah, I didn't think you would believe me. I tried but…" I shrugged my shoulders, "Like my Gram used to say, 'I'm wide in the eye'."

"What's on your mind?" Lance asked. I had no one else to talk to and Lance actually looked like he wanted to know so I turned and crossed my legs in front of me facing him.

I told Lance I was thinking about home and how I missed it. That I realized I had been here almost a week and it felt longer than that. That I still hadn't been outside, I just walk from room to room and sometimes stared out the window. I felt like I wasn't myself and I didn't know how to get back to me, and I felt alone.

I was surprised I didn't cry, but maybe that's what I needed all along, to just talk about it so I could stop being a hot mess. Lance was very understanding and listened through it all, even telling me that maybe finding something therapeutic around here would help. I don't even know how long I talked but I felt better afterwards like a heavy weight slowly lifted little by little. It was like the fragile cracks were starting to harden up a bit.

Lance stepped out for a minute and I looked back outside, noticing the large yellow moon through tall trees in the distance. Opening up the window, I could smell wet grass. I didn't realize it had rained that whole time I had been talking, but it almost looked like the grass was glowing from the reflection of the moon, it was really pretty, like sparkling diamonds on the ground. When Lance returned back I had relaxed a lot. I still didn't want to go to sleep because I didn't want another nightmare, so I tried to think about something, anything, to get my mind off sleep.

"So what's your story, Mr. Tillis? We've been together for a minute and I don't know anything about you." I asked randomly, not thinking he would be open to talk about it, but I was surprised that he was.

Lance was born and raised in Kansas City, his dad passed away two years ago and his mom moved to Florida after she retired from teaching six months afterward. Starting as a rookie investigator with the FGA ten years prior, he worked his way up to being the youngest special operative of the department within five years. Lance got extra training with the Navy Special Forces that allowed him to be independent with permissions to receive intel that others couldn't. I asked lots of questions about his time as an operative, but he couldn't tell me too much because of confidentiality.

"I've done some things I'm proud of and some things that I'm not so proud of, but that comes with this line of work," he said. "You do what you have to do and have no regrets."

Lance decided a year ago that he was going to work his way out of all the physical aspects of his job and do mainly investigative work. This case was his first in his new role, I'm pretty sure this was not what he was expecting at all.

Other than the demanding job, Lance was just a regular guy. He was thirty-three, no wife, no kids. He said he was always trying to learn something new, "Never a dull moment in my brain," he remarked. He liked football and working out and his favorite childhood memory was flying kites with his dad in the backyard.

I was so surprised how regular Lance was. I guess I thought because of what he did there was no life with it. By Lance opening up to me about personal stuff with no hesitation, it made me feel comfortable about telling him more about me.

"I've always been a Texas girl, proud of it, too. I can't see myself really living any place else, well maybe one day, but it would be somewhere else south."

"Are your parents in Texas too?"

"They live in Texarkana 'living the dream' as they say, on thirty acres of farm my dad got after my Gram passed away." I didn't see them as much anymore because I started having a life. When I first moved out, I was there every weekend, eating dinners and helping around with some of the cattle. One day my mama came to me and told me if I was gonna be there all the time I might as well move in and quit my job. I drove back home that night and decided that there was a point to being on my own and that was so I could do my own thing. I didn't come back for months.

I loved my job at Land's Down Bar & Lounge. I had been working there since I left home at twenty-one and didn't plan on leaving anytime soon. That lounge was my second home and everyone was family to me there. I could play on that piano almost anything as my style varied depending on the theme needed for the night. I always gave it my all because I wouldn't have it any other way, even if I wasn't feeling my best.

"Do you ever play when you're not working?" Lance asked.

"Oh yeah, all the time. Music is my life; I'm always trying to create when I'm not at work. Something about it makes me feel alive. You do remember seeing all the stuff in my house and my slippers, right?" His brown eyes lit up and he quickly stood.

"Follow me." He held his hand out to help me out the rocker. We went down the stairs and entered the sitting room. The far corner held a large storage closet. Lance opened the doors and I walked to turn on a light. When I turned around, Lance was pulling a white sheet off an ivory acoustic piano; it was beautiful. Its black and white keys were perfectly aligned as if no one had touched them in years. I lightly placed my hands over each one. Though it made me instantly miss my grandmother's piano in my townhouse that I spent hours playing music on, I was excited to see it here. Unfortunately, it was way out of tune.

"Do you have the tool kit for the piano somewhere? I can fix this like right now," I said excitedly.

Lance shook his head. "I don't think I've ever seen anything like that around here." I thought for a moment. Most acoustic pianos came with tool kits, and most people I know keep them close by to not lose them.

"Have you ever checked under the piano?" I asked.

"No, I never had a reason to look."

A moment later, Lance crawled out from underneath the large instrument.

"I would have never thought to look there." I took the bag from him and opened it up. Everything I needed was there. It was as if they had never been used. Within an hour and Lance's help tightening up screws and wires, we were done. Satisfied, I sat there admiring my handiwork while Lance went to wash his hands. I heard each tone in sequence. I only had a dull throb in my wrist but nothing excruciating when I tapped the keys. I could hear a melody just as clear as day, and I began playing.

The piece that flowed through my fingers was something I wrote called 'In the Blues'. I usually played it when I was troubled, and seeing my current situation, it suited just fine. I closed my eyes and felt the pulse, each stroke took me further away from everything. I could see colors behind my closed lids, blues, purples, reds, and greens flowing with the tones. It was just me and the notes dancing in my head on the piano. When I ended, soft clapping came from behind me.

"That was really nice," he said.

"Thank you." He came over and leaned on the piano. "Seriously, how did you learn to play?" He listened as I started tapping random notes and explained to him about how from the time I was little, I had an ear for music. I used to walk around the house humming random notes, and making music with anything near me, including Mama's shoe boxes. Daddy picked up on it and thought it would be a good idea to put me into music classes. I fell in love with the piano and never looked back.

"I always wanted to learn how to play chopsticks, it always looked so easy on T.V." I smiled at him and moved over on the bench. I loved teaching the piano as much as I loved playing, it always made me feel good knowing I helped someone create.

"Well come on over, unless you have something else to do."

Lance looked at his watch, "Let me see…nope, nothing to do at all." He said smiling and sitting down. I had him look at the keys as I explained the basics.

"There are eighty-eight keys on a piano, but no key has the same tone no matter where you go, whether up or down. The notes playing with the keys read as A, B, C, D, E, F, and G." I had him press a B note high and a B note low.

"See, same note, but in a different key." He nodded his head in agreement. I went over chopsticks and about thirty minutes later, he was playing it by himself. After three runs, Lance stopped and looked at me.

"I never thought I would ever learn that, you're a good teacher."

"Well, you're a good student," I smiled back.

"Why thank you, little lady," he replied, tilting his head as if he were tipping a hat.

"Little lady… that's funny." I said laughing at his reply.

"You know, this is the first time I've seen you smile and laugh since we've been here, I'm glad to see it." I looked at him then pointed to the beautiful piano in front of us.

"Well, I can tell you this definitely helped, it's always been my therapy, but you may have helped a little too. Thank you for being a good ear earlier." Lance nodded as he explained that's what he was there for. He asked if I wanted something to drink and went into the kitchen. I looked down at the keys and began to play with one hand as he walked back in the room and sat on the couch. I played and played and played, completely forgetting about everything else.

W. Owens

Lance

Lance knew that Meek was beginning to make mistakes, mistakes they don't normally make. The alerts he had been getting is that with the bodies at Maxie's house and the car about two hundred fifty miles away with two men in the trunk, they were certain the group was taking notice. Lance had been too near for comfort before with Meek but this was one of the closest exchanges he had ever been in with them in such a short amount of time. The fact that they were so desperate to find Maxie made Lance think that they weren't going to stop, and if they weren't going to stop, he wasn't going to stop protecting her.

He was a very light sleeper so when he heard covers rustling in the room across from him, Lance knew she was having it hard sleeping again. He waited some time then realized it had been a while since he heard anything. Entering the room, he noticed her soft face looking out the window, those curly locks flowing off her shoulders. Boy, he wished she wasn't so beautiful, but she was. Lance watched her expressions as he talked about himself and then her about her life. He got to learn more from his roommate and she learned more from him that anyone else had in a long time.

The atmosphere of the cottage changed after they talked and Lance showed Maxie that piano. The look on her face was of excitement and listening to her play those notes was amazing. You could tell she would be a good teacher one day because of the way she took her time explaining to Lance how to play something as simple as chopsticks. Everything about it made perfect sense, from the explanation of each note to the placement of hands.

The rest of the night, he sat and watched her play with a peaceful look on his face. He now understood how this was her therapy.

Maxie

Having that piano here was a lifesaver for me. I was starting to slowly feel back to my normal self and it made me happy. The sad and depressed Maxie needed to be gone a long time ago.

I was even finding it easier to talk to Lance as he was not only a good listener, but in getting to know him, I found that he was a pretty nice laid back guy. Having my guard up about him didn't feel necessary because he never gave reason for me to feel uncomfortable, if anything, Lance had been trying hard to make me comfortable. I was open to talking about the case freely now without being upset, and that was a big step for me considering all I've gone through.

The desk was stacked with open folders. Yellow highlights painted the sheets and red handwriting was scribbled about. There was a board hanging on the far wall by the window holding a map with pins and strings connecting to one another. I could see little pictures of faces behind thumb tacks. Small monitors were stacked on top of each other along a wall showing what looked like the outside of the property in different spots.

107

"Wow," I said looking around the room. Lance continued to stare down at papers in front of him. I pointed to the stack.

"That's a lot."

"Yes. There have been more arrests, so I wanted to update all of my paperwork. By the way, I called your job and told them the company you won your vacation from extended your time and you would be out for a while longer."

"Were they ok with it?"

"Yeah, your boss was fine, especially when I said you picked him up jelly beans." I grinned thinking about the smile Tyler would have had on that call. I looked around again at the setup.

"Tell me again how in the world you're able to know everything that's going on back home if we are so far away?" He pulled out a drawer in his desk and there were cell phones scattered about.

"I have multiple burner phones that aren't traceable so I can get information I need from sources I trust if I need to make a call. I also have programs on my computer and a laptop that's encrypted with access points."

"So let me get this straight, you only come here when you're off assignments but you have all this equipment like Fort Knox? Doesn't seem like relaxation to me," I said shaking my head. Lance was quick to disagree.

"It's all precaution, you can never be too careful these days." I looked at each screen, no movements, not even a car.

"How far away are we from everything?" I asked.

"The closest neighbor is a mile down the road." He went back to the screen. *So, in other words, if there was a fire, we were screwed...great.*

"None of this makes any sense to me, all the electronic stuff," I said staring at blinking lights and buttons and images.

Lance showed me the security system and how it worked from in the room. I sat in a chair right next to him trying to see everything he was explaining to me. Ten camera screens stared back from different points of entry, as Lance called them, from the property. Each camera was set at one hundred and eighty degrees so if someone were to come from the right or left, you would see them. There were also cameras at the edge of the property hidden discreetly. Had I known this days ago, I probably would have been more relaxed. No one would be able to get to me without being seen.

"Now look, if ever you wanted to use a certain camera, you push this button first." He pointed to a small green button on a huge control board in front of the screens. I leaned in further to see it.

"This one?" I asked putting my finger on a button to the left.

"Yes, that's the one. The toggle next to it changes the angle of the cameras in case a strong wind moves it off the setting." Lance motioned for me to grab it, and after moving it around, nothing happened to the screen.

"Not quite, here let me show you." Lance put his hand over mine, then pushed the button in front of the third screen. I noticed there were separate buttons in front of each one. We moved the camera around a bit then Lance started to put it back where it was originally. It was then I realized his hand was still over mine because I was making the same arm motion as him. The more I took notice, the more it felt weird being this close. While Lance was focused on putting the camera back into the spot he wanted, my mind went to how unusually close we were sitting. His aftershave was light and fresh and filled my nostrils and I began to stare at the side of his face. *He smells really good. His face is smooth too, kinda reminds me of melted milk chocolate...*

"See, it's not too hard to do." When I didn't say anything, he looked at me, or should I say, caught me staring at him.

"I got it," I said a little too quickly. There was an awkward moment between us, me being slightly embarrassed and Lance realizing my eyes were on him. I finally blinked and Lance moved his hand away. I cleared my throat and stood up.

"So thanks for showing me this. I'm gonna um, I'm just gonna go get something in the room."

"Yeah, sure," Lance replied. I walked out and to my room and shut the door behind me.

Alright Maxie, get a hold of yourself. What's the deal girlie, cause I think you liked that a little when he touched your hand. What's wrong with you? That ain't ok. I shook my head and gave myself a few minutes to get it together. Taking a deep breath, I left the room. I found Lance still in the office looking at the pictures of the men that were still at large. I was so glad he started talking because I didn't know what I was going to say.

"The shipment that was planned on the day of the shooting was found three days ago in an old abandoned warehouse on the other side of the city. There were hundreds of firearms and cocaine packages recovered. FGA doesn't know who Meek was sending them to but they are hoping this will be the big break they need. They are still recovering evidence as we speak."

I felt good knowing that whatever information they had could help get some more people. The quicker they got more, the quicker I could get home. I grabbed a stack of mugshots on the desk and was looking again at the unfamiliar pictures, and a thought crossed my mind.

"You talked before that it was possible someone inside FGA could have leaked information out. Maybe FGA didn't have someone on the inside, maybe I was followed to begin with?" Lance looked at me, his mind catching up to what I had just said.

"That certainly is a possibility. I've been looking at just FGA and not anything else at this point. So far it's been a dead end. What are you thinking Maxie?" Lance walked around the desk to where I was sitting in the chair and leaned on the edge with his huge arms crossed. I tucked my feet underneath my legs in the chair. I was staring at the pictures from the hospital.

"Well, the driver of the second car wasn't one of the men you were fighting in the park. I know for sure because you didn't know there was a third person until I told you at the hospital, and the guys were bloodied up too. What if this guy was watching from the time you found me and brought me in? He would have known every move I made from the hospital to home and could have called it in on me. He could be the same person in the car FGA was chasing the other day." I paused for a moment before continuing.

"Maybe he realized at some point I wasn't there and my place was being staked out. I mean I don't know, but that makes sense to me. I still don't remember what he looked like or anything but, it could be him."

Lance turned around and searched the desk. He grabbed a folder and pulled papers out. Reading for a moment, he looked back to me.

"FGA did pull full prints from the driver's side of the car that was chasing you and partial prints from the passenger side. If we match one of these guys here in the pictures with what was recovered, that's a big thing. I know you said you don't remember what they looked like, but I want you to really think about it, even a small detail would help." I wanted to help, but I didn't know how. I stared down at the floor and took a deep breath to think back to that day.

In my mind, I always ran through it all fast, so I wouldn't linger on it, but now I needed to remember. There was the dark car crashing, Mr. Bates on the ground, the men coming back, the man who flipped him over…

"The man, one of them turned Mr. Bates over and said something to him." Lance stood up straighter.

"What did he say?" I closed my eyes and thought long and hard.

"I don't know, my windows were up. I never heard anything, but I know he said something." I could see myself just getting to the park.

"When I was running I turned around. Someone was bald with a mustache. Wait! Someone was yelling something about me, something like 'get her'." I waited another minute but couldn't think of anything else. Lance had a concentrating look on his face, then jumped up suddenly and searched through the photos, grabbing a couple. He scanned it through the printer then started typing fast. I sat there in silence as typed and clicked away. After what seemed like forever, Lance looked up.

"We should know soon if there is a match from the photos I sent through and the prints in the car. The prints don't belong to anyone we have so far in custody, but something you said gave me an idea." I could see hope in his eyes as he looked back at his monitor.

After sitting a few more minutes waiting for him to say something, I decided to go get some air. I put on a light jacket and went to the back doors. Opening one, I sat down on the rocking bench looking out at the yard. I had finally got enough nerve to go out to the porch a couple of days ago and started to spend most of my time between there and the piano. The porch had a roof over it and a wood banister that ran three sides. Besides the bench, a small plastic table was next to it, then a grill in the far corner.

Even though I was relieved the driver might get identified, questions flooded my brain. *If I had been followed since day one, and this guy had not been caught; that means I was still in danger? Did he know I fled the state? Does he know where we are now and just waiting to make his move? When everything was over, would I still always look over my shoulder? Would I feel safe?* That was the hardest thing to think about. I continued to look out, trying to see as far away as I could, but the questions clouded my thoughts more over.

"Mind if I join you?" a deep voice asked. I looked up to Lance standing next to me. I don't know how long I had been in my mind and I was still muddled with thoughts but I moved over so Lance could sit down. I looked down at my hands then back up to the cobblestone path.

"I've looked out in this yard every day since we've been here and finally got enough nerve to get out on the porch, but that's all. Isn't it sad? I finally made it outside but not too much further than where I already was. I'm still too afraid to leave and go out in the open. How I wish I wasn't, how I wish I would just go and smell those flowers over there or even walk barefoot in the grass. It's crazy how one thing changes how you see something that's so simple." I sighed.

"To know that there could be someone out there watching scares the hell out of me. It takes the joy out of admiring all this beauty. And I know we are far away, but still it's the thought of it all. What makes it worse is I'm the one that put this in my mind." Lance turned and rested his arm on the back of the bench. He looked at me carefully.

"I don't expect you to act like nothing is going on because a lot of things are happening. You are going to have times where you are ok and you are going to have times where you are like you are right now. I will do everything I can to help you as best I can. I don't want you to think that you are a prisoner here. This place isn't going anywhere so if it takes you a little time to get comfortable then so be it. Please know that you are one hundred percent safe here."

"But how can you be so sure? If they found out about me before, who's to say we aren't being watched right now? They could just be waiting to make a move." Lance placed his hand on my leg and patted it lightly.

"You have to remember Maxie this may be all new to you, but it isn't for me, so you just have to trust me on this. No one is out there."

There was something I saw when I looked at Lance that told me he was telling the truth. I didn't want to ask anymore; I just had to tell myself that I would be fine. Nothing has happened here and it will stay that way. We have cameras, fences, alarms and Lance and we have been fine. I sat back and put my head on the bench. It was easy to agree, but it wasn't so easy to let it go in my thoughts. I saw Lance looking out in the distance then he got up and walked down the steps. I followed his movements to a flower bed. After looking around for a moment, he bent down and got a yellow tulip. Returning to the porch, he handed it to me.

"Nature can still come to you even if you don't go to it." Looking down at the flower I softly touched the petals. I closed my eyes and inhaled deeply and for a moment, I didn't have any fear. *That gesture came on time. Maybe it won't be so hard after all, to destress myself.*

"Are all Special Operatives as nice to their witnesses as you are? Cause I can't see them being nothing but hard to deal with." Lance smiled and touched the flower I had in my hand. He looked at me with a smile in his eyes.

"No, but I'm not your ordinary operative... I have a heart and feelings." I laughed and looked at him, the sadness slowly diminishing from me. "I see, I got a good one, dully noted."

We sat and talked for another hour or so about just random things and it was nice. Once we headed inside Lance checked for an update and information came in that FGA got a hit on a set of prints to match one of the men in the photos.

"Eugene Spell, forty-five years old. He has a long rap sheet, including assault with a deadly weapon, and kidnapping." I looked over Lance's shoulder as he read the rest of the information.

"As far as they can tell, this guy right here is one of the top dogs. He's been around for a while and has done just about everything imaginable in the illegal game."

"So this is the man who was driving the car the day they came after me?" I pointed to the picture sitting on the desk. Lance shook his head.

"No. These prints were matched up from the partials on the passenger front side." Frowning, I looked back at the picture. I never saw this guy get out of the car. *Someone else was there?* Lance explained that there was another set of tire tracks on the scene at the park. *So, that was probably a getaway car.*

"The prints for the driver matched up as well. An address popped up too, they are looking into it as we speak." I slowly got up and went to the poster board on the wall staring at it.

"So what happens now?" Lance got up and joined me in front of it. He moved some of the threads around the spider web of a map. There were names and small pictures and maps with circles on them. I didn't even ask what the board was about because there was so much happening on it.

"We wait and see if they catch Spells and the driver then see if we can get more information that can get us closer to solving this case." The calmness I felt earlier was beginning to thin as a thought of yet another person being out there turned my nerves.

W. Owens

Lance

He couldn't quite finger it, but there was something about Maxie that Lance was drawn to. He had been denying it for days, but being in close proximity to her, Lance knew he was very much attracted. Keeping a poker face was beginning to get harder, especially when he touched her delicate hand under his because he immediately felt a jolt. Lance had never felt this smitten before, he didn't even know how it happened but it did, and there was nothing he could do about it, which compromised things.

Infatuation is one of those things that usually turns into nothing. You think you like someone because of whatever the circumstance was that brought you together, then it fizzles out just as quickly as it came. For Lance, it was one more thing on his growing list of issues…he thought he beginning to like Maxie.

Lance had been looking at the paperwork for hours. Mugshots and reports and sticky tabs were scattered all over the desk. He thought he had rubbed his entire beard off as he stared at down at all the words. Though he was glad that progress had been made from all the arrests, something was missing he couldn't quite wrap his brain around.

It took the fresh pair of eyes from Maxie to open his and he was grateful for it. Pinpointing someone of top rank from Meek means that they were one step closer to taking them all down. Lance was really excited about the days that would follow. When FGA got back to Lance and told him that it was Eugene Spells sitting in the passenger seat of the car, the excitement changed to another emotion, worry. Lance knew that things were going to get very complicated when all of this ended. Spells being there meant that things were as serious as he was starting to fear.

Outside, Maxie revealed to him why she was hesitant about being out in the open. He definitely understood and he also knew that even though he wanted her to trust him fully, that may take time as well, they were still somewhat strangers to one another. The best he could do right now was be there for her and that way, when she was ready to go out there, he could be the support she needed.

The more time Lance spent with Maxie, the more he was beginning to find that his hope of following those goals he set was looking better and better.

The first step had been easy because it was in his nature to be polite and respectful, especially to a woman. His mom always told him no matter what, always, always respect. And with the exception of a few instances, he was able to keep that in tune. Step two had been more difficult and still a work in progress because as much as he tried to convince her that everything was ok and she was safe, he could see she still had reservations about it.

Three seemed to have come before two because Maxie had become more comfortable than in the beginning with him. The first couple of days together in her house and here in the cottage were a little dicey but she had been slowly coming around, thanks to the piano in the cottage, which made everything easier. Even Lance was feeling himself becoming more relaxed. He knew he needed to watch his boundaries with that, but it was hard because there was something about Maxie that brought out the natural side of him, not the serious work side all the time.

Four was still a work in progress no doubt. It was going to take all his strength to get her to trust him, but he could see things were changing and that gave him hope. The one thing Lance needed was for Maxie to not have any more doubts about him or the situation. Knowing Eugene Spells is in the picture, Lance knew that if he told her everything about him, she wouldn't take it too well. On one hand, if he never said anything and she found out, it would be bad all around. On the other hand, if he was up front, it would be almost starting back at the beginning and Lance couldn't bear doing that to her, with all that had happened.

He didn't want a complication like that to add to everything else as that one thing could jeopardize the progress slowly being made. The more they communicated and got along, the better this would be for everyone, especially Lance.

W. Owens

Maxie

"Are you ready?" Lance asked.

"Yep, let's get this show on the road." We were in the kitchen; I was sitting on the counter next to the sink waiting for Lance to take out the rest of the stitches from my arm. Most of them fell out on their own, except a couple stubborn ones. I was planning on heading to the exercise room Lance had set up in the place so I could get into some rehabilitation. My wrist was mostly out of the brace too, but still had a little ways to go but I was excited.

There were small clippers and tweezers by me. Using alcohol, Lance wiped down my arm. As he clipped and pulled the rest of the threads, I got anxious. The last one came out and Lance felt the scar then grabbed some hydrocortisone cream. After he was done, I jumped off the counter and headed in the direction of my next task: exercise.

In the small room, surprise covered my forehead. Ten arm curls that should have been a piece of cake were straining. My plan was to start with three-pound hand weights and work my way up, but at this rate after ten, that was a long way away. Three sets of ten for everything I told

Lance when he suggested a light routine. I couldn't back down now because I already committed so I dropped the weights, took a deep breath, wiggled my arm and wrist, then went back to it. The second set was worse than the first and I was starting to get frustrated. When I went to the last set I made it to five before stopping.

"Dammit! It's not supposed to be this hard!" Lance came and stood in front of me, but I turned away, pissed off at myself.

"Look at me, Maxie." I stared at the floor, then put my hand on my hip angrily looking in his direction.

"You still have some healing to do. It's going to hurt, that's why I mentioned doing something lighter, plus your wrist isn't one hundred percent. How about you take a break for a minute then get back to it, but slower." I gave him a dirty look and walked to the other side of the room fuming. I was madder over the fact that he was right, I tried to do too much too quick. In my mind, I imagined it was going to be great, but the minute I felt the first stretch of muscle, I knew.

Thirty minutes later I sat down on the carpet and I stared at the ceiling nearly defeated. My arm, for the most part, was fine; it was my wrist that was giving me the most trouble. It had been just a couple weeks since everything happened but I could still feel tightness when I moved it certain ways and I didn't like that it wasn't better. A shadow appeared to my right and Lance was there. He handed me water and put a cool pack to my wrist.

"Thank you," I mumbled. I think he could feel my frustration because he started to try and make me feel better, at least I think that was what he was trying to do.

"One thing I learned over time is things that appear simple aren't always that way. Playing the piano and doing weight exercises are two totally different ways you are using your arm. The biceps," he pointed to the large part of my upper arm, "and the triceps," pointing to the back of my arm, "all work for strength. Your wrist was probably severely strained which is why it still feels like you can't use it fully without discomfort. It's going to be like that for a while because of that. I sat there moving my wrist all around, feeling where it was tender. *Of course, my luck.* Lance took my wrist and started to massage and stretch it out carefully. I could feel some of the tightness ease a little and my body began to relax. I was once again impressed with him.

"How do you know so much about this, special training or something?" I asked after a minute.

"I told you, I like to learn new things."

"Well, hell, is there anything you don't know?" Lance didn't respond, only smiled. He stood and held his hand out so I could get off the floor. I was still irritated which made me think about other things bothering me. Upstairs in the bedroom, I stared through the window watching the sun trying to break through bright white clouds.

Maxie darling, you need to put those big girl britches on again and get your ass outside. There's nothing to be afraid of, no one is out there. It's been almost two weeks, stop being a chicken.

I paced the floor, glancing here and there outside. No matter what I told myself, I still felt nervous as I left the room and made my way downstairs and out to the porch. Looking at the three steps that fell onto a cobblestone walkway, nerves screamed in the back of my head as I stared straight ahead. Convincing myself to stop the foolishness after a few minutes, I slowly made my way down. The hard part now was moving away to walk along the path.

It seemed like hours but it was only seconds before I stepped away and made my way to about the middle of the path. Flower beds lined up on either side of me as I reached the middle of the yard. Satisfied with where I was, I looked around. The yard had about thirty feet of grass on either side of the flowers. The fence was black wrought iron about eight feet up and there were trees and bushes along every inch of it. About a quarter of the way on the left sat a white round table with two chairs.

I only stood for a couple moments longer, but I was happy and relieved I got that out of the way. I figured it would only be a matter of time before I made it to the end of the yard at the gate, but for now, I wanted to pat myself on the back. I thought about the garden I saw and how I could give it some TLC when I came out again, trying to prep myself up with motivation.

I took a deep breath and relaxed a little more. *It's a start Max, be proud of this. You're making progress.*

Turning around, Lance was on a step leaning on the railing with his arms crossed, a soft smile on his face.

"Damn, nothing gets by you does it?" I asked walking towards him.

"No." I made it to the steps and leaned on the rail opposite of Lance. I looked back in the yard; it really was beautiful.

"What made you decide to come out here?" Lance asked.

"Well, I couldn't stay confined forever and turn into a hermit. I was also frustrated with myself for listening to the fear instead of your words that I was safe, so you may have helped a little too."

"Well, that's my job."

"What is?" I asked.

"To make you feel safe." I looked at him, smiled, then turned to go inside.

"Well, I'll mention it to your boss. Keep up the good work, cause I'm almost there."

♫

Going out there and facing my fear put me in a good mood, and nothing was wrong with being in a good mood, especially since I was tired of being in a foul way. I had been at the piano for a while, playing nothing in particular, just enjoying the vibe around me. I was hoping I would have

more days like this going forward because I liked the good
ones. Lance walked in with a laptop and sat down on the
couch. Not saying a word, I kept playing, I was in a groove
frame. I could tell he was lazily typing because I didn't hear
the keys tapping away like normal. Every now and then I
would peek up and see him looking out the bay windows. *I
wonder what's was on his mind?*

I zoned out and played with notes floating in my
head. I saw yellows and light blues, whites and pinks
dancing around. I eventually opened my eyes and looked
over to see Lance asleep, with the laptop still in his lap. This
was the first time I ever saw him actually sleeping, and I
played a couple more minutes before I closed the top down
on the piano then walked quietly over to him and carefully
moved the laptop onto the coffee table.

I knew Lance hadn't been sleeping much, what with
trying to keep me sane, checking security cameras, and
staying updated on the investigation. Lance was a very light
sleeper too, a creak in the place and he would be up, ready to
go. Exhaustion catches up, even to the best of us. The mere
fact he didn't move when I took the laptop told me the
sandman finally gave him a K.O.

Turning the stereo low, I decided to occupy myself by
making something to eat. By the time I finished, Lance still
hadn't moved so I cleaned my mess up and grabbed an
entertainment magazine. When Lance started to finally stir, I
was on my stomach on the floor flipping through my second
magazine tapping my feet in the air to the beat of a song
playing. Lance opened his eyes, looked around a moment
then checked his watch sitting up quickly.

"Hey sunshine," I said. Lance turned in my direction on the floor and blinked.

"I thought for sure I'd catch you snoring. That's the longest time I've seen you sleep ever. Oh and don't worry, the place didn't burn down."

"Sorry about that," he said stretching a little then standing up. I closed the magazine and looked over at him.

"Why are you apologizing, you do have to rest. That applies to everyone, even a machine like you, besides," I said getting up, "You're pretty peaceful when you're asleep and not on the serious channel." I went to the fridge and got out the pitcher of tea I made earlier to pour myself a glass. Lance came over to the counter and sat on the stool.

"What's that?"

"That," I said, "is sweet tea." Grabbing a glass, I put in some ice cubes and poured him some. He took a sip and looked at me. *Expression of enjoyment...priceless.*

"See now, that's Texas Sweet tea, it don't get no better than that sugah." Smiling, I leaned over on the counter, watching him drink. I thought about earlier when we were in the sitting room.

"When I was playing, I saw you looking out the window a couple times, you seemed far away. What were you thinking about?" Lance put his glass down.

"Nothing really."

"Oh come on now, I could see a lot from where I sat and that was more than nothing. I don't bite you know." Lance smiled.

"Yes you do, especially when you get upset, you've got a mean bark little lady."

"Well then don't get me mad, and anyways, we're not talking about me. Ah, come on now, who am I gonna tell," I waved around.

"Just not going to let it go, are you?"

"Nope." Lance tapped the counter and I refilled his glass.

"Something you were playing reminded me of a place in Italy."

"You've been to Italy?" Lance nodded.

"Is it what they show it is like on T.V.? You know, all the water like streets and all that jazz?"

"Just about, and almost every building I saw was made out of brick." Lance stopped talking and I crossed my arms and gave him a look because I knew that wasn't all that he had been thinking about.

"I was on tour there for about six months. One of my partners told me about this coffeehouse that was about thirty minutes from base he heard about. I was thinking it wouldn't be anything like the places in the states, but when we got there, I was surprised. It was just right you know, like the lights were low, people were talking quietly, and the music, man, the music just made you forget about all the madness and relax…just like yours." Lance stared off for a moment, it looked like he was back where he was earlier. A soft smile was on his face, his dimples deeply creased.

It was nice to see this side of Lance as he opened up to me. The more I thought about it, the more I wanted to get to know this part of him. He really seemed like a cool guy, but he didn't like to show it too much. I knew we were probably going to be here for a little bit so while he had a mission to protect me, I decided my mission would be to crack the hard shell chicken egg and get to the soft center that I've only seen a couple times. I wanted a friend in this faraway place.

♫

I must have put the whole cottage in a positive vibes because when I grabbed crackers, fruit, cheese and carrots to take to the porch the next night, Lance came out and joined me with a pack of beer, that I apparently never saw we had. Looking around and taking everything in, it seemed like this was the first time since we got here that the both of us looked chilled out. To be able to really act regular, it never really happened, and that was mainly my fault. I just wanted to feel normal now, like nothing was wrong in the mess called my life.

I tucked my feet underneath me and faced Lance. For some reason now it was as if I saw him for the first time in plain sight. There were just a couple flecks of gray in his low-cut hair. A lined beard framed his face and came up to the top of his hard jawline. There was also a faint scar that went along the top of his left eyebrow. Looking down at his hands, they were strong, hard veins tracing up his arms. I was busted out again for staring as Lance caught me for the second time. I cleared my throat taking a sip of beer. *Maxie!* A warm breeze came through blowing my hair back off my face. I grabbed it and made a loose plait to the side. As I finished, I saw my scarred arm.

"It looks good," Lance said. I nodded and felt the outline of it with my finger.

"It doesn't feel bad either," I replied. He leaned up and ran over the slightly raised skin, his touch bringing a slight tingle up my spine. *Did I just blush at this touch?*

"This is pretty good," he said. I could still feel his gentle touch as he turned to face me and rested his arm on the back of the rocker. He paused before he spoke.

"So how have you been doing Maxie?" I wasn't expecting Lance to ask me that question so it took me a moment to respond. *How have I been doing?* I grabbed a piece of cheese and nibbled on it.

"You know, I thought I would have been losing my mind by now being here still. Don't get me wrong, I do miss home and work, but I think not being here alone is what is helping me." Lance looked down at the plate and grabbed a cracker and cheese.

"Well hopefully it won't be too much longer, but I do want you to be comfortable here. I'm pretty sure we are well done with formalities so we might as well make the best of it." I was surprised but was glad Lance said that. It made me feel better knowing I wasn't the only one that wanted to feel normal. I figured this would be a good time to get Lance to open up more so I decided to jump right into it. I stared at the cobra on his forearm and pointed.

"When did you get that tattoo?" Lance looked down and smiled lightly. I could see his eyes change up a bit.

"I was in combat training for a year. The sergeant got a kick out of picking on me all the time. I'm not sure why, but he never thought I would cut it. He used to tell me that if wanted to go home I didn't need to pack because I didn't deserve anything in my hands." Taking a sip of his beer, Lance stared off past the trees taking his mind back to that time.

"No matter what I did, it wasn't good enough. My arms weren't in proper form, or I wasn't quick on my draw, or even if I took down my opponent, it was wrong. I got to the point where I wanted to give up, I didn't want to serve if I kept getting berated."

"Damn," I said, imagining how that must have felt. Lance nodded, but soon, the darkness in his eyes slowly changed to peacefulness.

"I ended up calling my dad, told him I was done and I wanted to come home. He told me something that day I would never forget. 'Son, you don't let words of others change you. You know who you are because you know who you are. That's someone who is trying to break you down to the core, make you believe you can't, when you know you can. You let words build you up, you let words make you a better man.' Words I needed to hear."

"I started training myself for hours after the day ended. I would look up everything I could, I even started meditation. Weeks passed and the more I studied, the better I got. The guys started to call me Cobra because I got stealthy. I finally looked up and realized he stopped judging me; instead, he was acknowledging me. The day I graduated was the day I got this tattoo to remind me of that time, because even though it was the hardest times, it showed me what I was capable of."

Here I am, a small-time girl in a bind and there's Lance. *No wonder he is the way he is. What else could he say that would surprise me more?* I grabbed another beer popping the top, my eyes now wandering to Lance's face.

"So you've been a lot of places, seen a lot of things, your life is full of everything. It makes me wonder, what's the one thing that you want?" Lance shrugged his shoulders and looked as if to say 'I don't need anything.' I shook my head hard.

"There's got to be something, think about it. Everyone has had something that they have seen and they think, man I wish I could have that… I'll be honest if you be honest." Lance laughed heartily then looked out towards the trees in the distance. I could tell he was contemplating something.

"Companionship."

My eyes lifted in surprise, "Really? I find that hard to believe." Lance smiled and leaned back, bottle in hand. I thought I could sense a little sadness creep up as he started talking.

"Well, believe it, being in my line of work can be a lonely job. Sure, you meet a lot of people, but you can't call them friends. It gets worse if you have friends who don't understand why you have to be away on assignments for weeks at a time and not hang out. You kind of give up after a while and hope that one day you run into someone who understands it."

"I guess I didn't think about that; it's probably hard to be in a relationship too on top of keeping friends." I looked down at my glass, feeling bad I even asked. It was just crazy to me that this man sitting next me that has gone through things that I couldn't even imagine felt lonely. The sadness lasted a moment longer on his face until he blinked and focused back on me.

"What about you?" Lance asked.

"What about me?"

"Are you in a relationship?"

"I thought we were talking about you?"

"Well little lady, the subject has now changed." Laughing, I put my glass down on the side table, grabbed another one and curled back up on the rocking bench. I thought I interrogated him long enough.

"Well sir, I don't have a boyfriend." Now it was his turn to look surprised.

"And why not?"

"Because I don't."

"Why?"

"Are we playing fifty questions now?"

"No. Just maybe five or six questions." By now I'm giggling and I was pretty sure at the rate we were going with revelations, the beers would be gone soon as I took a sip then twirled a strand of hair around my finger.

"To answer your question, I'm in a part of my life where I want to get a little serious and not casually date anymore. I think I'm ready to find the man who wows me."

"What do you mean wow," Lance asked.

"Like great personality, caring, funny, likes to have a good time and enjoys being with me. That's what I mean by wow. Seems like everyone sees me as a piano player and nothing else. I'm more than that you know...I guess I want companionship too." Lance put the beer to his lips and gazed out past the gates.

"I can see that you are more than just a piano player Ms. McHill and its refreshing, even when you're mad." He glanced over at me and winked.

"You just won yourself some brownie points," I said tapping his shoulder. Lance smiled, showing those deep dimples, which now made him look more good looking than he already was. He started rubbing the back of his neck nervously, which had me wondering what was wrong.

"Well…that's good to know and a relief you don't have anyone special," he said.

"Why?" I asked questioningly.

"I knew your boss would want to know who was calling you out for extended time off, so instead of you talking to him, I told him you were handling some things but he could let me know because…I was your boyfriend." I almost coughed up my beer.

"You're kidding!"

"He already met me remember, so it made sense to me at the time. Plus," he continued, "I thought I wouldn't want anyone to see you and think you were available, especially since I'm right by your side, that just wouldn't work." *I'm glad he's so good looking or else I'd be upset about it.* I scolded myself for even thinking like that about him.

"So I take it we should play on the lines of boyfriend girlfriend if we come across anyone?" Lance looked at me. I thought I saw a little nervousness on his face.

"Unless you don't think it's a good idea?" I looked out at the blossoming trees at the end of the yard. *What's it gonna hurt threading along? It's not like I'll see a lot of people anyway. It'll definitely stop the "who is he" questions... I'll play along.*

"Since you are a charming fella and have taken very good care of me, I will revoke my single lady card for the time being." I threw up my hands. "Well doggone it, this is how dating starts these days?"

After the beer outside was gone, we continued to talk. It was great, we chatted about everything under the sun. I truly believed it was something we both needed, a break from all the craziness that had become the current situation. I finally told myself that it was ok to still enjoy and smile, and even though I was confined in this place, I could still make the best of it. The sadness didn't have to be there all the time. It also felt that there was a growing friendship that had formed between us the past couple of weeks that I was finding myself enjoying more and more.

Lance asked if I could play a song before we "shut the lounge down for the night." I chuckled and we went inside. By now we were both feeling pretty good but I don't think either one of us really cared. I didn't know he was going to sit next to me but he said he wanted to see firsthand how the magic happened. He told me I could pick the song, I told him he could help me play. I sat and waited for the melody to come to mind. I showed Lance what I would need him to play and that he would know the song before the chorus.

"If Only," came to mind. It was my favorite song because for one thing, I had written it, and for two, because I put a lot of emotion into it; simply put, it was a beautiful piece. I wrote it two years ago and had dedicated it to all those people who thought they needed love in their life to be happy. The night I played it at work, a radio DJ by the name of James Knight was in the audience. He gave it airplay for his new hot local talent segment on his show which turned into my first single ever released to radio.

I got a quarter of the way through when Lance looked at me and smiled. I soon became lost in a wave of notes and colors, this time reds, purples and pinks, all that I felt flowed through my fingers. With my eyes closed, I could hear Lance's keys and they weren't bad at all. My favorite part was the end, it held so much that it always brought me close to tears. I was still in the zone when a hand softly touching mine brought me back to the present.

"Absolutely beautiful."

I don't think he was talking about just the song the way he looked at me. I stared back and this time, didn't look away searching his face.

W. Owens

Lance

He was surprised at her skills on the piano; he would have never believed she played for a living but he could see why. The way she ran her fingers across the keys was amazing. He could hear each note and each melody was as clear as day. All the times he had listened to her was a treat and this night was no exception except that he was sitting right next to her. He studied her as she played, watched her fingers run, watched her face relax. Being this close to Maxie as they sat, he could see all her features and he liked what he saw.

Maxie had smooth skin, her hair was loosely pinned up, he was beginning to like her with her hair like that, but then again, he thought she was beautiful however she had it. Her hands were delicate and she had thin fingers. He could see a small birthmark along her jawline close to her ear. The woman was sexy. She wasn't overweight, but she wasn't thin, she was just right.

Lance was thinking the attraction he thought he felt was just due to the fact of being alone for so long and now being in the space of a beautiful woman like Maxie. It didn't help that they got along and she was growing more

141

comfortable in his presence. As the days passed, Lance could see that he was also being more of himself with Maxie, though he couldn't believe he admitted that he was lonely to her. Lance wasn't sure if he did it because of the couple of beers he had, or if it was because he was throwing himself out there, but it was done and he couldn't take it back.

The more Maxie played the more he felt drawn to her. Those notes felt like they were speaking to him, he couldn't explain it other than he wanted to be close to her. When Lance placed his hand on hers he felt it again, just like he did in the office that day when he touched her. She was just as beautiful as the song she played for him and he didn't want to shy away from it anymore that night.

Maxie

They caught Meek members at the Texas/Mexico border in Laredo. After the vehicle was stripped down, thirty pounds of cocaine and marijuana were confiscated from the tank, the side door panels, and under the storage compartment console in the front seat.

There were also AR-15's, a box of hand grenades, bullet proof vests, and other weapons. The grenades had a serial code on them which fortunately linked the stash to the shipment container FGA was looking for.

Lance said everyone had their preliminary hearings and at the arraignment all criminal charges were listed. At no bail, their lawyer advised them to plead not guilty in hopes of coping a plea deal later for other arrests. This meant that I had to stay another thirty to sixty days here until trial.

"Not guilty!? Are you kidding me? They killed Mr. Bates, they came after me and tried to kill me and they've got the nerve to plead not guilty. Why the hell does that make sense?"

I was pacing the floor outside of the office in the hallway. Lance was trying to calm me down to explain to me that with all the evidence they have, it won't matter because they'll be in jail for a long time.

"Maxie, there is no way they're getting off that easy. It's just not possible, they have too much stacked against them. Everything still has to go to a grand jury but even if they get a deal, I seriously doubt they will ever get out of jail. We've been ready to take them down for a long time." I kept pacing, my mind was reeling. I stopped halfway through the hallway, and sighed.

"It's going to all work out, you'll see." I leaned back on the wall, thinking how I could end up being away from home for months.

"There is some good news out of this. FGA talked to your parents. They gave the clear so you can give them a call if you like from one of the phones, but keep it short." That was the only thing that made me feel better about everything Lance told me. The fact that I could finally call my parents. We got up and headed into the office. Lance grabbed a phone from the drawer and turned it on. I dialed the number from memory.

"Mama?" I called out as the voice on the other end picked up.

"Maxie, baby! Lou, it's Maxie!" she yelled out. "Hang on honey, let me put you on speaker phone so Daddy can hear too." I leaned back on the desk as I heard Mama push a button. Daddy's booming voice came through loud and clear.

"Baby girl, how are you?"

"I'm good Daddy." I could hear him grumbling under his breath.

"This world I tell ya, it's going to the shitpot. That's why I gots old Betsy on my hip just in case…" Mama cut him off.

"She don't need to hear that foolishness now, hush!" I could hear Mama fiddling around with something.

"They said you're somewhere with a Ranger or something and you can't go home? Honey Bee are they treating you right, are you getting enough to eat? I can make something and then have some of those FIA guys bring it to you. I know they aren't feeding you right." My parents, they are the 'Southern Special' as I called it, but I loved them so much.

"Mama, he's a Special Operative not a Ranger and it's FGA, but I have enough to eat, I promise." Daddy was fussing again in the back. "Baby girl you need me to come get you, cause you know I will." I heard rustling in the background then it got quiet. I walked past Lance in the office and headed to my room.

"It's just me Honey Bee. I left your daddy in the other room. Nevermind him, he's just upset this happened to you is all. Now tell me something, are you really ok?"

"Yes Mama, I'm fine, a little homesick but hopefully this will be over soon and I can get back."

"And that fella they put you with, is he respectable?"

"His name is Lance, and yes he is respectable." I looked behind me and smiled. I suddenly heard my mama sniffle and blow her nose.

"That's good baby, that's really good. Well, honey, I won't keep you cause I know you can't stay long on but we love you and glad you're ok. I'm gonna keep praying for you and you keep praying too, things will work out. You tell that fella to take good care of you. You need me, I'm just a phone call away Honey Bee." I could feel tears welling up in my eyes from hearing her voice. *What I wouldn't do to get a hug from you right now. I wish you were here to talk to me.* I suddenly felt like a little girl who was homesick from camp and couldn't go home yet.

"I love you, Mama," I softly spoke.

"Love you too, honey." I hung up the phone, wiped my eyes and turned around to give Lance the phone back. He put it in his pocket as I went into the bathroom to get some tissue. Talking to Mama made me miss home even more and I felt lonelier than ever being so far away from everyone I knew. I had been doing good for the most part until just then. A few tears fell down my cheeks but I wiped them away and cleaned my face before going back in the room.

"Could you just stay and keep me company for a while?" I asked.

"Of course."

"I don't know, maybe we can just like watch T.V. or something up here in the room? I don't really feel like being

146

by myself. Talking to them got me feeling a certain way now."

"Sure."

I grabbed a huge blanket from the chaise and unfolded it while Lance went to put the phone away. I sat in the middle of the bed then clicked on the T.V. He came back in the room and sat next to me pulling up a chair. I tried to relax into the pillows that were propped up behind me. *Man, I'm glad he's here cause that call got to me.* I looked at the T.V. screen just as a movie started up, but I don't know what it was about because I soon fell asleep.

I hadn't had a bad dream in a while so I'm sure what happened earlier in the day triggered it. I only remember before I woke up there were hands around my neck squeezing the life out of me. I was scratching and hitting but it was no use, as I felt my last breath I could hear Lance calling my name. Catching my air in near darkness, he was standing over me. It looked like he must have come in the room as I could see him breathing a little hard. I had to sit up and lean forward to the bed taking deep breaths.

"Someone was choking me and I couldn't breathe, it felt so real." I immediately leaned forward and he held me tight. I felt like I used to when I was little and Daddy would come in my room. He would hold me in his arms and rock me to sleep. I felt like that little girl again, vulnerable. I stayed that way for a while with Lance trying to calm me down.

"It's ok now," he said. I took a deep shaky breath.

"I'll be right back." He started to move away but I held his arm with pleading eyes, tears brimming again.

"Don't go." Lance didn't hesitate and came back to me. He brushed hair from my face softly and lightly touched my back.

"You should try and go back to sleep Maxie." I nodded out of exhaustion and sat there looking around. Deep breath after deep breath I tried to bring it down, then I moved back in the bed slowly, sliding over and motioning for him to join me. There was no way I wanted to be alone in the dark having a nightmare like that. I could sense a little hesitation from him as I turned on my side and I felt his body slowly ease down.

"Ok?" he asked. I curled up to him as close as I could until I felt his bare chest on my back. I was still fidgety until Lance put his arm around me. My body relaxed more and more until the shivers disappeared. I couldn't believe something as simple as the conversation earlier about Meek then talking to my parents would stress me out. *Maybe it bothered me more than I thought. Maybe I was still scared, maybe...* My mind was fogged with thoughts that I tried to clear out of my head.

"You are a lucky lady," Lance said after time passed.

"How so?"

"You are the only witness I've been in bed with."

"I'm sure there were others you could have done this with."

"Hell no," he said chuckling softly. "Gary who was 6'5 and three hundred pounds; no thank you, I'll pass." I laughed lightly.

"Besides, I'd much rather be with a beautiful woman like yourself." I laid there for a moment, thinking about what he said. I turned on my back and looked at him through the dim light coming from my clock radio.

"You don't have to make me feel better by saying that. I'll be ok, really."

"I wouldn't lie about that." I felt flutters in my stomach as I decided to make a revelation myself.

"You're a pretty good lookin fella yourself you know." There was an awkward silence as I bit my lip trying to read him. We looked at each other through the darkness, neither one of us talking because no one knew what else to do or say. I wasn't sure if put my foot too far out of not, because he wouldn't say anything, so I closed my eyes and took a deep breath. I could still hear his deep voice in my mind through the quietness of the night and I felt him lightly brush the top of my hair away from my face and softly place his hand on mine. I slowly relaxed and fell into a dreamless slumber.

I felt the sun on my closed eyelids and snuggled more in my blanket. It was nice to feel so relaxed waking up for a change. Because I was halfway on my side and halfway on my stomach, I stretched my legs out and wrapped my arm around a pillow. I sighed and dug my head deeper into it. Something touched the small of my back gently. My eyes fluttered opened and I realized that was a hand and, my head was not laying on a pillow but something else. I could hear his heartbeat, it's mellow pace in my ear. I stayed motionless with my eyes wide open, I knew I should have moved but I didn't. I wanted to stay right where I was because honestly, it felt good and I felt safe in his arms.

After arguing in my mind on if I should move, I reluctantly sat up and looked at Lance with big eyes when he stared back at me looking like he had been up for some time. *Oh, did he know I was awake?*

"Well I must say, for such a little lady, you sure do snore like a bear." My face flushed and I raised myself up more, "Oh man, sorry I fell asleep on you."

"Don't be sorry Maxie, I'm not." Creases appeared in the corners of his mouth.

"You're not?"

"No. I just woke up a while ago and you seemed so peaceful I just let you sleep."

"I was really comfortable," I replied. Lance looked at me and smiled.

"I could tell." I stood up and stretched. Lance stood up and did the same. I turned and looked at the clock on the mantle-11am.

"Well damn, it's almost afternoon! It's been a long time since I slept heavy like that." I spoke over my shoulder, "Must have really needed it." I stood in the middle of the floor looking around still trying to wake up. Lance came closer to me.

"Everything ok?"

"I'm good, I just thought if I slept more like that more often…"

I came face to face with a disheveled mess in the mirror on the opposite wall. I grabbed my hair and tried to push it down.

"Why didn't you tell me I looked like I put my finger in a wall socket, holy shit!" Lance laughed, "Who am I to judge? If you didn't notice, I'm pretty sure I wouldn't win best dressed." *His clothes weren't that wrinkled, but it didn't matter.* I looked around the room and walked to the closet.

"So I'm going to change then head out back, those flowers need some serious tending to out there. I'll come down pretty soon." I glanced over at Lance and he wasn't looking at me, he was staring at me, it seemed different than normal.

"I'll meet you out there in a while." Lance turned and walked across the hall to his room.

I managed to get myself together but I was thinking about last night and how it seemed to make me feel better and how the more I thought about it, the more I kinda of liked everything about it. I was beginning to think that maybe Lance was growing on me in a different way and I was debating whether or not to talk to him about it. On one end, I was nervous, if I told him and he didn't respond, I'd look like an ass and we still had some time left here. But then I could go about things like they are supposed to be in this whole situation. On the other hand, I was hoping he would say he might like me a little even though I knew it was wrong. In the end, I decided I should probably say something, just get it out there in the open.

My heart was beating pretty fast with each step down the stairs. Lance was standing near the window in the kitchen looking out and turned when he heard me approach. He stared at me not saying a word for a moment before clearing his throat.

"I was thinking we could eat outside on the back porch for dinner later, it's supposed to be really nice out there." I nodded chickening out on talking to him.

♫

A beautiful afternoon and I had been cleaning up and watering flowers in the backyard, Lance was cutting the grass. My mind wandered off and I was back in the park, with the trees and moss and darkness. *Lance was off in the distance. I was running after him because someone was behind me. I could hear footsteps close to me. I finally reached him and he embraced me. The footsteps stopped. I could hear his heart beating; I could feel his warmth.*

"I'm so scared," I said. "Please don't leave me, I don't want to be alone." I could hear Lance speak soothingly, his deep voice in my ear.

"I've got you, I'm here."

"Don't let go," I said holding him tighter.

"I won't," he whispered. I looked up, the both of us staring into each other's eyes. Lance lowered his head, his face getting closer to mine, until I could feel his breath. His lips touched mine. The footsteps stopped and all the darkness disappeared.

I didn't know I had turned and was in Lance's direction while my imagination went off in left field. I knew it was a daydream, yet inside, it seemed too real.

"You say something?" he yelled out. I didn't realize I had turned in his direction in the middle of the daydream.

"What?" I pretended I didn't hear him. He shook his head and finished up. I had my back to him and made it to another section of the flower bed when the mower cut off. I dared not to look again since I almost got caught the first time. *Don't stare Maxie, you'll probably creep him out, then everything will be all weird, like it isn't already. I know he has those washer board abs that looked like what Gram used to scrub her clothes with. Oh, I need to stop, this ain't right, this...*

"Are you..." I jumped in surprise spraying him with water. I zoned out that much that I didn't hear Lance come over to me.

153

"Shit, I'm sorry." I tried to turn off the nozzle but it was stuck and Lance grabbed it. The nozzle cap busted, water went all over me and all over him. I yelled out because it was so cold and jumped back and fell right on my ass. Lance threw the hose on the ground to run and turn it off from the house. It was wiggling all over the place and I was on my hands and knees, scrambling on the grass, slipping everywhere with the hose following me around like it knew I was struggling. The water finally stopped flowing out and I sat there on the ground drenched.

I tried wiping my face which was pointless so I did what anyone would do...I busted out laughing. The more I looked down at my puddle of water, the more I laughed. I mean really, what else was I supposed to do. *And that's what the hell I get. I probably looked like a wet dog.* Lance jogged back over and I was still laughing. I waved him off that I was fine and he stood there, a small smile forming on his face.

"If you wanted to cool off, you should have just said so," Lance said chuckling.

"Well, hell," I said laughing and throwing my hands up.

Lance went inside to grab towels and I managed to stop laughing enough to get off the ground and head to the porch. Wringing out my shirt and hair, I made it to the steps just as he opened the door and stopped, in his tracks. It didn't dawn for a second why he stopped until I felt a chill. The shirt was clinging to my body, it was cold, my bra was red, and everything was showing. He handed me a towel and tried not to look down but it was hard not see what was in plain sight.

I'm a pretty outspoken person but at that moment, I couldn't say a word because while he was looking at me, I was staring at his chest again. My heart started to beat a little faster and I could feel flutters in my stomach. I needed to move away or something quick because I was feeling like I didn't want to go anywhere. I looked down then I looked up and met his eyes. The flutter happened again. *Dammit Maxie, move it!*

"I'm just gonna...my room," I stumbled out.

"Yeah, me too." I wrapped myself in the towel and ran up the stairs, trying not to track water on the floor.

In the room, I walked to the bathroom and took off my clothes to dry off then change. The more I thought about it, the more I realized that yes, I felt a vibe going with Lance; and yes, I kind of liked it. I would have never thought I would say that, especially about Lance. He would have been the last one I would think that way about, but to be honest, I missed having that feeling of attraction for someone.

It had been almost a year since the last time I was in a relationship. When I would finish my sets for the night at work, I normally sat in the back in a favorite little spot to people watch. One of the bartenders at the lounge had taken interest in me and he would come over when all tabs were cleared out and chat with me.

Josein Pada was from Peru and had the sexiest accent I had ever heard. Gray eyes and dark skin, he was sensuous.

He had only been in the states for two years and was trying to buy a building to open a restaurant somewhere in Texas.

"Ma, I tell you truth, nothin makes love to the mouth like my food. I cook for you one night; you see what I mean." Even though I was a skeptic, I tasted his picarone desserts and I was reeled in. Josein would bring in different foods for me to try, which then turned into me going to his place every chance I got to eat. Flavors I had never tasted burst in my mouth and I was in love with it.

We started to hang out more and more, even when food wasn't involved. The dancehalls saw us a lot and man that Josein, I had to keep up with him! A fine man with a sexy accent who could cook and dance his ass off, I was sold.

We went out for a couple months and it was a good time, but I could tell after a while he was distracted with his restaurant stuff. I'm always the one to say follow your dreams so I wasn't too bummed out when Josein said he was leaving the lounge because he found a place in Houston to open up and he wouldn't have a lot of time to work there. We agreed to part ways but I asked him to send me food from time to time cause that definitely didn't have to end.

Getting out of the shower, I wrapped myself in a towel and walked to the closet. I found a pair of black skinny jeans and a long striped shirt that hugged all my curves. Admiring myself in the mirror, I was thinking to myself how Josein was missing a good time with these hips of mine. Realizing there was nothing left for me to do to distract myself any further, I paced the floor. I needed to talk to

Lance, but I didn't know how to start the conversation. I headed downstairs.

I grabbed a beer and sat on the couch, pulling the coffee table close enough to reach the pieces to a jigsaw puzzle I had been working on. I used the remote on the table to turn on the stereo in the sitting room. Carlos Santana's "Smooth" came through the speakers.

Looking at my surroundings, the stools and counter, the music, the drinks, and the piano in the corner made it feel like I was back at work and I was enjoying myself on a break. Moving some pieces around from a puzzle I had been working on, I took a sip of beer and glanced around. I actually felt a little lonely not seeing Lance after a couple minutes. I'm so used to him being around all the time that it felt part of my norm now. That got me thinking how I went from hating this whole situation to liking Lance being around, but there seemed to be more. It's like I was catching myself be a teenager who really liked a boy in class. I was pretty sure I was starting to like him.

As if he knew I was thinking of him, Lance came down with his laptop to the couch and some papers. I knew he had switched over to serious mode so I was trying to put a couple more pieces together before playing a few riffs on the piano. He told me that he liked when I played while he worked because it was less stressful, and since I loved to play I figured it was the least I could do. A couple minutes passed and he still never picked up the papers next to him, I could see he was concentrating on something. Curious, I leaned over to see what he was looking at.

"That's not work," I said pointing at the screen of a pretty landscape.

"No it's not." I scooted up closer and leaned in.

"What are we looking at?" Lance glanced at me and smiled.

"I was checking emails and one of those vacation package promotions came up for Morocco so I started looking at it. I was there about three years ago so it caught my eye." I put my finger on a picture that popped up.

"Casablanca?" He nodded and started to pull up more pictures. There were stone roads and deserts and beaches and little villages and snowcapped mountains. A little something for everyone.

"It's gorgeous! And you saw this in person...I'm jealous right now. Next time you decide you wanna go to Morocco, think of your friend Maxie as a plus one."

"Excuse me, going there isn't cheap. If I'm paying for it, what am I getting in return?" I grinned and cleared my throat.

"Me."

"Is that so?"

"Yep. I won't let you down, It'll be fun. We could sight see, and those hot air balloons are calling my name in that picture right there. Oh, I bet their dancing is exotic." I got up and swayed my hips back and forth to the music playing in the background. Lance's eyes watched me as I turned around and moved my arms around slowly.

"I could teach you some moves, and we could paint and drink wine. What do you say?" I heard nothing so I looked over my shoulder.

"Are you looking at my ass?" Silence.

"I hope you are, cause this ass needs to go to Morocco." I turned around and looked at him putting my hand on my hip. Lance looked at me and grinned, those deep dimples showing out.

"I'll take you anywhere you want to go if you move like that again." I laughed and plopped back down next to him looking at the screen again. *Ok now I think we are flirting... just a little.*

♬

Dinner that night was put outside. Grilled steak with an onion gravy sauce, dinner rolls and a salad. We talked and laughed like we had known each other for years. I never brought up the conversation I wanted to have because it was such a good time, and I didn't want to risk ruining it.

Lance looked down at his watch then off in the distance a before he turned and suggested we start cleaning up.

I walked inside to the stereo on the mantle and turned the volume up, grooves flowing through and followed us into the kitchen.

"Ok see now, this song is jammin." I spun around as I grabbed dishes and headed to the kitchen. Another good mood evening and it felt nice. We talked as Lance washed and dried the dishes and I put them away. Every now and then I would bump his shoulder to the beat and ask him to hurry and he would bump my shoulder back and ask me to slow down. It was a good time for sure.

Taking the stack of dry plates, I had to use the stepstool to put them away. I put them on the top shelf and pushed them back a little too far, so stepping to the edge of the stool I got on my tip toes to try and pull them back forward, but the stool slid from under me and I started to fall. Almost immediately powerful arms grabbed me. I opened my eyes to a pair of beautiful brown ones. I felt completely frozen and couldn't stop looking at him taking in all the details of his face. Lance stared at me as well.

"Thank you," I said softly.

"Anytime," he replied.

The music was still playing in the background; I could feel his heartbeat and mine begin to pound rapidly as his body stayed pressed against mine. My hands were wrapped around his neck. I looked in his eyes again; there was no mistaking what I saw looking back at me, and I'm sure he saw the same thing in my eyes... heat. Lance slowly pulled away and that's when I realized I had been holding my breath. I moved my hands from his neck to the top of his shoulders. Very slowly, I could feel my hands slide down his chest as I was getting close to the floor. My whole body tingled at this point.

Of course, neither one of us said anything to each other about it, but I thought it was pretty clear; there was an attraction, and it was brewing. For me, it took that small time to realize I was feelin Lance a little more than I should.

There was a cracking sound that broke the trance we had on one another. Looking down we could see pieces of glass he dropped when he caught me.

"We better get that up," I said out of breath, my head swirling. Silently, and carelessly I began picking up the broken pieces and cut the inside of my hand. I cried out in pain, Lance turned on the sink and put my hand under the water. He pulled it out and looked closer at it.

"Go sit in the chair." I sat down and he returned from the bathroom with the first aid kit. I watched him pull out tweezers, alcohol, cream and a band aid. He pulled a sliver of glass out, then cleaned and bandaged it up. Lance starred down as his hand lingered on mine longer than normal, handling it gently then lightly bringing it up to his lips. "Good as new."

"Thank you…again."

"You're welcome…again." Once more, I could feel that connection from minutes before. I wanted to say something but I just didn't know what.

When you are around someone for an extended amount of time, things change. You get to know them, you begin to relate, you become familiar to mannerisms. You can also become attracted to one another in some way, whether it be romantically or just a bond. It had been on my mind as of late that because of the circumstance that has placed us together that we created a relationship with one another of sorts.

I know that it is part of the job, to protect me and make me feel comfortable, but there has been something about Lance when I've been close to him, that makes me want to stay even closer. I've become more drawn to him and this night confirmed it for me. Something was definitely growing there and I was beginning to think the same could be said for him.

Lance

Lance had days of restless nights thinking about the lady with the smooth nutmeg skin and jet black curly hair that took his breath away the first time he saw her. There was something about her, and not just the fact that she was a main witness in a murder investigation. Though Lance had been on assignments just as long with others, this was different. He had been racking his brain over and over about what he had been feeling, and what he had been feeling was Maxie McHill. The attraction was getting stronger, she was on his mind all the time, even when he went to sleep he thought about her.

This wasn't how it was supposed to work, and as much as he tried to keep it professional and didn't want to jeopardize what his mission was, it was slowly turning personal. Lance had been thinking about what it would be like hold her like a caring person would, then thought he already was, whenever she needed that comfort. Then he thought about what it would be like to kiss her, because Lance thought if he could, just one time, but he already did that too, when Maxie had the nightmare the night after talking to her parents. She had been soundlessly asleep and started stirring and mumbling. Lance could only make out bits and pieces but the one thing he did hear was "Please don't leave me."

She didn't remember, he's pretty sure of that but he did and he'd thought about it ever since, feeling her soft lips on his when she sat up and came closer to him. Since it happened, Lance wondered what it would be like when she was awake.

Maxie

We were in the exercise room wrapping up a
workout. It had been almost a week and no one was talking
about what happened in the kitchen. The elephant was in the
room and no one wanted to go near it, but it was there,
looming overhead. We had been acting like normal like
nothing ever happened. It made me wonder if it was too
uncomfortable or if it was that neither one of us wanted to
admit we liked it.

Running on the treadmill, my mind was going a
million miles a minute. Lately, I had been thinking about
Lance, a lot. I really liked him and I didn't know what to do.
True, in the beginning, I didn't care for him too much but
now, things were different. Everything was different. I got
to know him and in doing so I got to liking him. Since we
have been here in the cottage, things changed between us.

I slowed to a walk. I was drenched, I was heaving
and I forgot he had been in the room the whole time working
out. I hit the off button and I jumped off. Patting myself dry
I glanced over. Shirtless and muscles tight, Lance was doing
situps; he looked so good.

I laid on floor with my eyes closed. *Why was I making this such a big deal? Was it really a big deal? Yes, it was. Lance was here to protect me not like me and everything, but I wanted him to because I really liked him.* I heard footsteps and then Lance peeked over me.

"I'm good, I'm good." Lance got on the floor and laid next to me.

"What are you doing?"

"Thinking."

"On the floor?"

"Yeah." I kept my eyes covered, trying to let the fan cool me off. It didn't do much good since someone was so close. *Why does he still smell so good when he's been working out? Oh, my goodness!* I don't know why I was acting like a girl on her first crush but I was. *Lance is a smart good looking single man and I am a smart good looking single lady. What to do, what to do. The late nights talking, laughing. The comfort of his embrace, his touch, the flirting...I'm losing my mind. We can't do this, but I want to do this. Dammit!*

"What are you thinking about down here on the floor?" I had no problem telling what's on my mind any other time so why not now? *Here goes nothing, what the hell. I mean, worst case scenario is he wasn't gonna react, right? It's not like anyone would know, besides we've both been a little flirty with one another.* I turned to my side and faced him, then quickly I backed out, again.

"I was thinking this was a good session, but I'm glad we're almost done." *Chicken!*

"Well let's try and wrap this up then," Lance replied standing up and motioning me to join him. I knew this time finishing up should distract me from where my mind was going. I decided to altogether put my mind on something else to pass the time away.

"Did you always want to work in a job like this?"

"I knew I wanted to serve somewhere, I just didn't know what branch," Lance stood up and grabbed the arm bar. He put grips on it and placed it on the doorframe.

I got off the floor and approached the bar. The plan was to hold my body weight for ten seconds, then twenty, and end with thirty.

"Was your dad in the service," I asked.

With Lance as the spotter, I gripped my hands around the bar. He lifted me up, my chin raising up to the bar.

"No, he was in a bad accident when he was a teenager so he had a bum leg. They wouldn't let him enlist." I dropped to the ground on my feet.

"How did that feel," he asked.

"Not bad," I said wiggling my arm loosely.

"That must have sucked not being able to go in, but if he was anything like you, it probably didn't slow him down."

I got ready to grab the bar again. I made the twenty seconds but it was harder than the first.

"Good Maxie, you got one more and that'll be it." Shaking my arm out for the last time, I gripped the bar. Sweat started on my brow. My arms started shaking. I could feel muscles weakening. I made it to thirty seconds right before my arms quit.

On the floor, across from one another with legs straddled out and feet touching, we took turns stretching our backs to cool down; Lance grabbed my arms and pulled me forward and I then did the same for him. We stood up and I grabbed his shoulder so I could bring each foot up behind me.

"Whew…made it." I wiped my face and shook my hand.

"I appreciate that," Lance said looking down at the drops that splattered across his chest. Laughing, I wiped again and flicked it off.

"Oh I'm sorry, let me move." By now, I was cracking up.

"Hey!" He cried and poked my rib a couple times making me jump out of my skin. The one thing I never handled well was being tickled and he just hit the worse spots.

"Interesting," Lance said raising his eyes. I saw a sly smile form on his face. I realized my reaction was the worst thing I could have done. I backed away from him with my hands out and maneuvered around equipment trying to put distance between us.

"I see that look on your face. What you're thinking isn't necessary."

"I think it is."

"It would be mean and you aren't a mean person. Look, your chest is dry now." I was hoping I could squeeze between the elliptical and the wall then out the door, no such luck. In desperation, I grabbed a towel hanging on the bench and tossed it in his face making a break for it. I got caught in the middle of the room. One arm held me and the other started an assault on my sides and stomach. I shrieked and was wiggling like a worm trying to break free knowing it was going to be impossible. We fell to our knees on the mat and I curled up in a ball, laughing so hard tears streamed down my face.

"Oh my God, stop! I can't take it, I'll do anything. I'm dyin', oh my God," I said in between laughs and tears.

"Here's the secret...I'm real mean," Lance spoke in my ear. He grabbed my thigh and squeezed, and I squealed. The tickles lasted until I stopped fighting and fell limp with another battle lost. I was sore from laughing so hard and the tickles so I stayed balled up, but managed to raise my hand.

"You win, you win, I promise!"

"That's what I thought," he said, grabbing the towel on the ground, handing it to me. I wiped my cheeks, trying to catch my breath.

"My, my, tears of laughter. Mission accomplished," he said laughing. I laid there still catching my breath. *I should throw this in his face, he's smirking over there. Then again, bad idea.*

"So you're ticklish I see," Lance said standing up.

"Not at all," I said, reaching for his outstretched hand.

"Liar." I was pulled up and right into him. My chest was still heaving but it wasn't just because I was still trying to catch my breath from being tickled to death. I could feel heat rising in my body. We were almost the same as the other night, only this time I wasn't caught off guard by the closeness. *Maxie, girl you're about to say something, aren't you?* I tapped his chest with my finger. I knew what I wanted to say, I just didn't know what he would say.

"Watch yourself," I said teasingly.

"Should I?" he asked, pulling me even closer. *He responded alright, now what Miss. 'I wanna flirt'?* I leaned up and forward, close to touching near Lance's ear.

"You probably should," I said, "I'm starting to like this right here. That's twice…I might not let go next time." Backing from him I walked out the room, fighting to not turn back around and look at him. I could have sworn I heard him say something back.

"I don't want you to next time."

♫

I knew that my bold move put things in motion that I was hoping I didn't regret. Given the way Lance reacted, I was more worried about how far this would go. I'm pretty sure I was the one that caught him off guard so inside I was celebrating my first win, but I was also kicking myself in the ass for letting the young giddy girl in me do that.

I was walking down the hallway towards the stairs when Lance came rushing towards me later that afternoon.

"Remember the old couple I told you about who sold me this place?"

"Yeah," I replied.

"They're downstairs."

"What!?" Lance spoke quickly but calmly, "It's their last trip with the family before heading to an assistant living facility, they wanted to drive up here one last time." I nodded then turned back to the room, but Lance stopped me.

"Not allowed, little lady, we're going to go down there together. They have no clue what's going on, besides, I already told them I was coming up here to get you. We'll just make it work."

"Ok," I said, *This should be interesting,* as Lance grabbed my hand and we walked down the stairs. The couple was in the sitting room looking around. She had short gray hair that was curled tightly and wore a floral print shirt and teal slacks. Her husband was wearing a shirt with a palm tree on it and an image of a sunset in the background.

"Oh, Gerald it's as gorgeous as I remembered it, don't you think?" He nodded in agreement.

"Mr. and Mrs. Wilson, this is my girlfriend Violet." I squeezed his hand tightly and looked at him as to say, what?

"Violet, really?" I whispered through a smile before I reached forward shaking their hands. After the brief introduction, the men went in the sitting room while Mrs. Wilson and I went in the kitchen. She insisted that she make coffee because, "Nothing puts a smile on one's face like a fresh ground cup of Joe." I sat on the stool in front of the counter while she prepared everything.

"My, my, this hasn't changed a bit. Everything is still in place. Isn't this the coziest house you've ever been in?"

"Yes ma'am it really is." She placed coffee grounds in a French press.

"Do I detect a slight accent, Violet?" I smiled and nodded, impressed because though my parents have strong southern tones, mine was faint. Not everyone catches it right away.

She asked me where I was from and what I did for a living. The beginning of the best lie in the history of all my lies came out. I told her I was from Arkansas and I used to perform for some small plays throughout the state.

"Used to be?" she asked.

172

"Yes, ma'am. People just don't go to plays as much as they used to so, unfortunately, our productions slowly shut down. Lucky for me I kept all my pennies and had a good savings so I was able to take my time to think things through. I packed a bag and took off to choose my own adventure of sorts. Then this handsome man came along one day and swept me off my feet. He saved me really," I rambled on.

"What handsome man?" Lance asked entering the kitchen with Mr. Wilson at tow.

"That coffee couldn't be anyone else's but Grace's, it sure smells delightful," Mr. Wilson replied. I got up and grabbed four mugs, milk, creamer and sugar, then went over to the table to set everything up.

"I was telling Mrs. Wilson how after the play production company I worked for closed down I was trying to figure out what to do with myself then you came along." Mrs. Wilson walked around and poured everyone a cup. I had to direct it to Lance because I was trying to come up with my next part in my story.

"Oh yes, what a day that was. You had a handful of maps the and a pen in your mouth standing in the middle of..."

"Downtown Miami. I had just gotten in the city and was trying to find my hotel room. I was tired because I drove ten hours in," I replied.

"I was heading out from lunch, the wind had picked up. She wasn't paying attention when I walked by and she ran right into me, maps went all over the place," Lance said.

"We were chasing them everywhere, then I mis-stepped off the curb, he caught me." *Ok, that was kinda lame.*

"And then I saw her beautiful face." Mr. Wilson chuckled and nudged Lance's arm.

"Son, if I didn't know any better, I'd say it was love at first sight." Lance raised my hand and softly kissed it. I could still feel them when he pulled away.

"It most certainly was." His gaze was penetrating and I had nothing to respond back to because he was so convincing right then, so I just smiled.

We chatted around the table for a while because Mr. Wilson was very interested in my acting days. I was having fun in this world I had made up and I was able to ad lib for a while but then excused myself and Lance to get another pot brewing.

"An actress from Arkansas? You had that whole story in your head," he said. "If I didn't know any better, I'd say you were enjoying this." I grinned.

"Maybe, but I think you are too, Mr. Love At First Sight. You just jumped out the gate like that? Are you trying to top me?"

"Maybe," Lance smiled, dimples deep with enjoyment.

"Game on buddy, let the best actress, win. Oh, that would be me." He looked and nodded, clearly with a face that took my challenge.

We headed back with the coffee. The couple had moved to the couch and we switched everything to the small table, sitting on the love seat. Lance put his arm around my shoulder and I leaned into him. I knew that we were playing the part but something about how naturally we had fallen into step with one another like sitting there made me think back to those inklings I had been having about us. Nothing about this felt wrong at all, and to top it off, what we made up went along with our body chemistry.

Lance told them we traveled a lot in the past six months, the last place had been Morocco. I had to smile on that one because of the fact that I wanted to go there. I knew a lot of the places he talked about were assignment sites so it wasn't completely a lie, but he made it vivid enough that I was sucked in myself. *Dammit, I don't think I'm winning.*

Sometime later in the conversation, the Wilsons wanted us to go somewhere with them on a hillside. Because I had never been outside the gates, I had no clue what they were talking about and I got a little unsettled thinking they would surely figure everything out if I couldn't get it together. I wasn't sure if I was ready and had to excuse myself to gather my thoughts. Lance followed and pulled me in the exercise room where they couldn't see us and reassured me everything would be ok.

"It's past the gates but straight ahead about thirty yards." I looked back at the door and in the direction he had

175

been talking. This would be the first time I left the yard, I would be lying if I said I wasn't scared. It took me a moment to ponder the pros and cons of it all.

"You'll be just fine. I got you."

"I know you do Lance, it's just... How am I supposed to act this couple thing out if I'm on edge?" I heard the door open in the back. I looked at him nervously then leaned forward, taking deep breaths as he hugged me. Out in the open didn't sound inviting at all. On the other hand, I wouldn't be alone, three other people would be there, including Lance. I tried to convinced myself that I would be ok so I looked at him and trying to put on a big girl face, agreed to joining them. He went into the office to push the button setting the alarm. Coming out on the porch, I waited as Lance turned and locked the back door. I paused for a minute before I stepped down onto the path that led to the back.

We came closer to the crab apple trees I always looked at from a distance with gorgeous pink flowers on each branch. As we all walked by, I stopped and plucked one and held it in my fingers. I was so engrossed with the vibrant magenta color I didn't realize Lance was calling me until he tapped my shoulder and told me to look up. We were at the gate. I suddenly froze, fear rising in my throat. I wanted to turn around, I wanted to go back into the house. I was terrified. How did I go from being a flirt to a storyteller, to a scaredy cat in this short amount of time?

Nervously I asked, "What if someone sees me?" Lance stood in front of me putting my hands in his, squeezing gently.

"We'll take this slow, ok. I want you to close your eyes and take a deep breath for me." I nodded and did as instructed.

"I've got you, I'm here." I opened my eyes and looked at him. *He said that in my daydream.* I couldn't help but stare. *Or was I just hearing things?*

"I promise you're gonna be ok."

"Ok."

Holding on to Lance's hand tightly, we took about thirty steps out past the gate with the Wilsons well ahead of us. The faint scent of saltwater hit my face first. Another twenty feet and I saw the ocean in the distance just past some tall bushes. I didn't dart my head back and forth looking for someone, and I didn't run back into the house like I thought I would. I kept walking with Lance, my fear diminishing my body because now I was curious with every step.

At the top of the hill, there was a bench off to the right. The older couple went and sat there looking out. Mrs. Wilson took a tissue out of the pocket and dabbed her eyes as she smiled looking our way. We stepped away well out of earshot so that they could share the moment with one another.

Lance led me a short distance to the top of a beautiful landscape. Seeing this for the first time since coming here weeks ago, it was enchanting. The most beautiful place I'd ever seen laid before me. Sea salt washed through my nostrils and I looked out to a paradise. Miles of golden sand below bordered the cerulean blue ocean. Seagulls flew high looking for food from above the water and to the right, huge rock hills climbed high to the sky. The sun was beginning to set; purple, red and orange hues broke through the clouds and sprayed rays to the sparkling water. I closed my eyes for a moment and felt the breeze on my skin. I just stood there for a long time quietly looking out. My mouth was wide open, I was mesmerized.

"I thought you might like this."

"Oh my God." I turned to look at him, his face beginning to grow darker with the setting sun.

"I want to take this all in up here."

"Absolutely." I still couldn't believe I missed out on this because I was too much of a chicken to come out. Seeing this right here would have taken all my fears away. *Who could be scared with something like this in front of your face?* I looked over at the Wilson's sitting together.

"They look so happy. I'm glad they were able to make it up here again."

"Yeah, they do." He moved around and put his hands on my shoulders from behind and gently started squeezing.

"Are you good?" Lance asked. I took a deep breath and looked out towards the breaking waves nodding.

"You know I really appreciate you right now, more than you realize. I'm sure I've been giving you the blues and I wouldn't blame you if you were tired of me by now." He reached and took the blossom I still had in my hand and tucked a strand of my hair behind my ear with the flower.

"With such a beautiful face, never tired." I turned back at him, my mind was in overdrive thinking about this moment and what to do. I was in what looked like paradise with a man that was supposed to be my boyfriend but was really my protector from people trying to kill me. *Maxie girl, this is something else, not to mention romantic. Wow, how things changed during our time here.* Looking up at the birds swooping down, I chuckled lightly.

"I wish I could just keep you just right here in my pocket, that way you can jump out when I need you." Huge arms wrapped me up. I took my hands and placed them on his forearms, closing my eyes. This felt good and I didn't want him to let me go.

"Well, I can't fit in your pocket, but you've got me for a while when you need me, little lady." My body relaxed and I sighed under my breath. I looked back over at the Wilson's who were now staring at us.

"We pulled a very convincing act, you and me," Lance whispered. I could smell his cologne, it's fresh scent danced in the breeze.

"Take this on the road, after all, I am an actress now. I think I could win an award," I said as I put my head on his chest.

"I could win an award too you know. I did a good job." Lance said sounding hurt.

"You did pretty good," I said laughing lightly, "But I did damn good if I say so myself. Pretty sure they don't suspect a thing from me. Don't worry, you still have time to prove you're Oscar material so get creative, we still have a show to finish." I could feel our bodies move closer as he nuzzled my neck and his lips touched my skin. It was like electricity was filling up my body. I instinctively tilted my head. That was not supposed to feel that good, but it did.

I sighed deeply, telling him to watch himself as I felt his lips again. I don't think at this point either of us remembered we were supposed to be acting still, well, at least I know I wasn't. I turned my body and looked up at Lance as he put his hands around me. He looked different now, and it wasn't a bad thing. The way his hands felt was even different. I had to think about my words before I spoke again.

"That didn't feel fake...at all." He had a look on his face that told me everything I needed to know, but I wanted to hear it.

"That's because it wasn't." I stared over at the Wilson's who were deep in conversation, not paying attention to us again.

"There's something going on right now Lance," I spoke softly, standing there trying to read his face, waiting.

"You're right." Now it was his turn to look at me to respond.

"And I'm thinking back to the other day. I'm pretty sure I won't pull away this time," I said. Lance raised his hand and gently touched my face, his voice became real low.

"I want to kiss you Maxie, but I'm afraid if I do that, I won't want to stop." I closed my eyes and my heart fluttered as Lance pulled me closer.

"You know Grace, some couples," Mr. Wilson said, interrupting us, "Have a spark between them, that makes darkness turn into day, no matter how big or small the storm is."

"Oh young love," Mrs. Wilson said. "That looked like us many years ago Gerald." They smiled at each other as we broke our hold and came back over to them. Mr. Wilson went on about him and his wife of forty years, and how he knew she was the one as we listened intently.

We ended up staying out just past dusk looking up at the stars then out to the dark ocean. This was the most beautiful place I have ever seen. After a while Lance suggested we get back to the cottage so that the Wilson's could get back in town before it was too late. I ended up walking with Mr. Wilson and he talked the whole way while Lance had Mrs. Wilson's arm. I kept glancing over, I knew we had some talking to do after they left. That wasn't acting, that was real and I needed to know what we were going to do about it. To distract myself from Lance on the way back, my thoughts went to the Wilson's in front of me. To be able to make this trip one last time had to be something special to them. Before we got inside an idea formed in my head.

"Could I play a song for you two before you leave?"

Lance piped in, "It's quite a treat." They went to sit on the sofa, I walked to the piano nudging Lance on the way. He winked at me. Sitting down, I thought of a song that I felt tied everything together, "Unforgettable."

My hands floated over the keys as I heard the lyrics in my head, only they weren't in my head. It was Mr. Wilson's voice coming from behind me. I could recognize that baritone anywhere; he was *the* Gerald Wilson, the singer from Chicago what made his living with a quartet in the early 60's and 70's. I followed his music for quite a few years and had all his records. He was amazing, and I was out of my mind.

'That's why darling, it's incredible...'

I matched his pace key for key. I was blown away; never would I have ever thought I would play for someone like Gerald Wilson.

'Thinks that I am, unforgettable... too.'

Mrs. Wilson and Lance gave us a standing ovation. She embraced Mr. Wilson then told him it was getting late and it was time to head back to the hotel. He started to sing 'farewell, so long until we meet again', and we all had a chuckle. When we all reached the door, Mr. Wilson took my hand.

"It has been a pleasure, Ms. Violet. We shall meet again indeed. Mr. Roberts," he turned to Lance and shook his hand, "You hold on to her, this gal is one in a million, other than my Grace of course."

"I intend to," Lance replied.

I had walked back towards the kitchen to clean up as Lance was shutting the door. My hands were shaking with excitement.

"Oh my God, did you know who he was?! I didn't recognize him at all until I heard that voice and then it came to me. I met Gerald Wilson! Do ya hear me? I played a song for Gerald Wilson. Eeeeeeee!" I was smiling so hard my cheeks hurt. Lance took a coffee cup from my hand smiling and I jumped up and sat on the counter as he rinsed out the rest of the dishes. I rambled along about Gerald Wilson's music career from the time he started in Chicago, to when he had his final performance some twenty years ago in New York City. No one had seen him since that time.

"What made it so great was that he was a legend when it came to crooners and he never changed with the time like a lot of musicians did. He stayed true to himself and the music, oh the music." I felt like a schoolgirl who was just picked to play solo in the band.

"Vin is gonna flip when I tell him. Boy, I tell ya, what a day."

I watched Lance put the last cup up then turn around. He moved and stood in front of me.

"I'm glad you enjoyed yourself." I nodded hard.

"I sure did, like you have no idea. I gotta be honest, I…" Lance suddenly came forward and kissed me deeply. I lost my breath right there. When he moved away, I looked closely at him. The way Lance stared at me made my heart skip a beat. It was as though time was standing still. I put my hands around his neck.

"You just earned your award, but, no one's here anymore to watch." I stared in his eyes then I kissed him. What started off as short savory kisses, turned into long lingering ones. Lance pulled me to him and I didn't object. I parted my lips and felt his tongue taste mine as my arms rested on his shoulders and his hands held my waist. My body felt weak and I could feel myself falling back on the counter with Lance guiding me gently down. He moved his head and kissed my neck softly, then back up to my lips. I started to fall deeper into the passion that was rising inside of me. Our movements became slower and Lance finally stopped and looked at me. We were both breathless. He stepped away and I sat back up on the counter.

"Whoa," I said above a whisper, fanning myself off. My head was spinning; Lance was rubbing his head with his hand. I got off the counter and started rambling.

"I mean, I didn't know it was gonna be like that. Nothing wrong with that, cause I wanted to but, it's like, you know…ok did you feel that?"

"Yeah," Lance replied. And we both looked at each other. It took everything not to go back to him, this was all wrong, we both knew it. He's the protector, I'm the protected; that's how it's supposed to be. *But what if?*

I was biting my lip because I was fighting with myself. My body wanted him bad but my mind actually kicked in and told me it was a bad idea. I wanted him to follow my hesitation but I didn't. I needed a minute because what I was feeling was a lot, a lot more than I realized. Leaning against the counter a warm breeze was coming through the window. I just stared out in that direction.

"Come sit with me, Maxie." Lance moved to the sitting room and I sat down first. He sat and faced each other. We finally were honest with one another and it was the most amazing thing I had ever felt in my life, but what now?

Another breeze came through and I closed my eyes to listen to the rustling leaves. I felt soft lips touch mine yet again. I opened my eyes and looked squarely at Lance as he traced his fingers on my hand.

"So I guess we should talk about what happened now," I said.

"I think we already did that," Lance replied.

"If I recall, we didn't discuss anything."

"We discussed quite a bit right there." He motioned to the kitchen. I followed to the spot we were just at, the spot that changed everything. I took a deep breath and started talking.

"I thought maybe it was just that we had been up here for so long that was why I felt closer to you, but it never went away. It seemed like there was something that I knew was there." I looked at our hands then out the window.

"I thought that way too at first, but to be honest, I was drawn to you from the time I came and saw you in the hospital, it just grew into something more as time went on."

"Really?"

"Yeah, and the first night you played that song for me on the piano. I'm not sure I can explain it other than it just felt right, sitting there. When you lost yourself in that song, I could really see you. I was sitting there, and the melody was speaking to me. I was speechless."

"But we aren't supposed to be like this." I twirled a strand of hair around my finger.

"I know....I know." It was the first time I heard Lance sigh and seem uncertain.

"So I think there is a problem," I said. I didn't want it to be a problem, I mean we were both adults and it's not like anyone was here watching us. On the other hand, if this turned into a mess, the rest of the time together would be the longest time together.

"Does it have to be a problem? I don't think there has to be one. Eventually, I have to go back to my life and you have to go back to yours, but what about just doing now? Instead of hiding it, why not just enjoy the time here and see what happens." That surprised me that Lance said all that. I thought it would have been me saying that and him disagreeing. We both stayed silent for a long time. I weighed the reasons why it was a bad idea then looked back in the kitchen. There was absolutely nothing bad about what happened in there, other than we stopped. I wanted that feeling again. I longed for that feeling again. When I looked over at Lance, he was staring in the same direction I was, probably thinking the same thing I was thinking.

W. Owens

Lance

Lance noticed the subtle flirting started sometime after the incident outside with the water. He remembered seeing Maxie and couldn't do anything but stare at her beautiful body. He wished he wasn't feeling so crazy about her but he was and when she started responding in her own teasing, Lance played a little with the idea of showing hints, but he held back a lot, especially in the weight room when he fought everything not to kiss her right then and there.

For some reason that day seemed like the right time for everything and it couldn't have been more perfect than when the Wilson's showed up at the cottage. He knew it was a gamble that they pretend in front of the Wilson's but the truth was, Lance was never pretending. Everything about that time felt real, there was no pretend in that whatsoever and he knew it.

The awe in Maxie's face was priceless when she saw the scenery at the top of the hillside. When he placed the flower in her hair, and even though she was a pretty outgoing person, he didn't know how she would react to something like that. Things had definitely changed in the atmosphere but would his feelings get in the way of the main objective which is to protect his witness and help bring down this corrupt group if he told her how he really felt? And would she see him to still be her protector if things changed like he thought they eventually would? The only thing Lance never regretted or doubted was him kissing her, as he had been wanting to for a long time.

Maxie

A loud sound from downstairs startled me from in my room. At first, I thought it was in my head but I heard it again. I got up and went to the door. Opening it slowly, I looked across and saw that Lance's door was closed. The banging was louder so I followed it to the top of the stairs. I made it halfway down and froze; I could see shadows on the other side of the french doors to the back porch. *Oh, my God!*

Running back up the stairs as the door opened and someone came through, I shut the bedroom door and made it to the closet. Climbing all the way to the back and hiding behind clothes trying to make myself as small as possible, I was praying I wouldn't be found. There was nowhere to go except out the window and that was across the room. Trapped, I heard the door open, heavy footsteps were walking around. I couldn't tell if there was more than one person and I had to stifle a cry because beginning to heave.

"Maxie?" a deep voice called out.

"Lance!" I was so relieved to know it was him. He opened the door and saw me trembling, shaking, scared.

"Come here." Grabbing both of my hands he helped me up and out of the closet. I hugged him tightly. He had his gun out and a large duffel bag.

"I saw people about a mile up the road from the surveillance cameras on the edge of the property. I don't want to be stuck anywhere near here, let's go. I know how to get through to the main road."

We took off through the back door and down the cobblestone path. At the gate I turned around looking back only once, no one was there. I ran towards the hillside with Lance.

The path had small pebbles that were packed down for hikers, Lance led the way with his gun still drawn. I moved faster, trying not to slip, the ground keeping favor and not being rough. The huge trees made shadows that hid us from anyone seeing us. Once we got to the bottom, Lance grabbed my hand and together we made it along the beach sand.

I followed Lance another five hundred feet then we reached a clearing between the trees and the sand. He started moving branches and there was another SUV hidden. *No one just has a hidden vehicle on a beach, why would anyone do that?* Lance threw the duffel bag inside with us in the front and we took off. I looked back as we made it through a trail and then onto a road. I started to get a little on edge.

"We should have just stayed there, why are we going where they could see us? And why do you have a truck just hiding out like that?"

In Safe Arms

Lance didn't answer as we flew down the hilltop and made a right onto the main highway heading north. I noticed a black Dodge sitting on the side of the road sometime later as we sped away. Lance slowed by it and they pursued.

"Is that them? Are you crazy? Why are you letting them know it's us?" He looked at me briefly. The car inched closer and Lance brake checked them then slowed to a stop. My eyes bugged out.

"Trust me," was all he said.

Lance got out of the car and I stayed behind. A man got out of the passenger seat, the closer I looked the closer I realized he looked exactly like…

"Spells," Lance said.

"Well, so nice to see you, Mr. Tillis. It has been a while. I see your scar is healing nicely, brings out the color in your eyes." Spells replied. I frowned and looked at Lance. My heart skipped a beat when they shook hands. *What the hell is going on?* Spells looked at me and nodded. He looked older than the mugshot I saw. The weather had damaged his face badly. He looked like those head mobsters on T.V., tailored suit, thinning hair slicked back, big jewelry.

"You know, you could have called sooner and we could have gotten this taken care of a long time ago," he said pointing to me.

"I couldn't risk it. I needed to know everything they knew about us." Spells pulled out and lit a cigarette then took a long pull. And that's when it finally hit me, *Lance was with Meek!* They both glanced over. His driver walked to the truck, opened the door and snatched me out. My face of shock told it all, there was no way I could hide what I heard.

"I seemed to let a cat out of a bag, haven't I? Well, well let me give you a bit of advice sweetheart, you can't trust everyone with a badge. I must say I was impressed myself. An FGA agent who was assigned to take down a corrupt organization, only he was involved with them all along, that's good material." I lunged for Lance, but I was still being held by the other man.

"You son of a bitch! I trusted you!" I screamed at the top of my lungs. Spells came over to me as I was fighting to break free. He pulled a knife out of his pocket, the blade touched the side of my face.

"I would hate to ruin that pretty little face of yours so soon, we just met." I stopped moving, scared because I could see he wouldn't hesitate. He nodded to the driver and I was put in the back of their car.

"So what does she know?" Spells asked. Lance turned his back to me. The window was rolled down and I was close enough to hear their conversation but I strained my ears to hear it all.

"Not much, she was only able to identify a couple people."

"She didn't see anything in the store?"

"No." Spells got another cigarette and took a pull.

"Those cancer sticks are going to kill you," Lance said.

"Better me than you." Spells paused and looked down the road.

"You know Mr. Tillis, the one thing I can't figure out is why you've been gone so long, if she didn't know anything?" he said inhaling.

"There was a lot to cover up. Since I've been playing both sides of the field, I couldn't just walk away, especially since they put me in charge. I had to play it all the way through. Besides, this was a good way to make sure what she knew." Lance looked back at the car and I stared squarely at him, seething. I couldn't believe this whole time Lance or Mr. Roberts or whoever the hell he was, faked everything to me, everything. I fell for all of it and worse of all, I fell for him and that was the cruelest part of it. This was the ugliest betrayal and I was in the middle of it.

"If you hadn't sent those idiots to her house, this would have been resolved a long time ago," Lance said.

"You killed one of my best men there."

"If those were your best men, then you've got bigger problems than I do to get out of all this shit. I had to cover my ass, not a smart move. Including the two you had tail us when we left," Lance smirked.

"Choose your words carefully Mr. Tillis." Lance shrugged his shoulders.

"I had to make it real." Spells stomped out his cigarette and glared at Lance, then he grinned and slapped his back.

"I like that. Willing to do what's needed, I like that." They talked for a couple minutes then Spells got on his phone and made a call, then they all came back to the car with Lance sitting next to me in the in the back. Spells got in the passenger seat. The driver took the wheel and we got on the road. I said not a word while Lance and Spells talked about their next moves once they got back to Texas. There were more gun shipments coming in and he really needed Lance's help making sure the transactions were smoother with a new middle man since Mr. Bates was dead.

"He was too worried about his family in Mexico, wasn't being the businessman he was supposed to be with me. Mr. Bates got careless and screwed up an important shipment. But, seeing as we don't have to worry about that anymore, things should get back to normal."

"What about her." Spells turned to looked back, his face was stone cold.

"Now she knows too much," was all he said.

Oh my God, I'm going to die? I thought frantically as Lance turned in my direction. His look confused and scared me because the expression didn't make sense; he looked concerned. Lance touched my hand on the seat and I pulled it away. Looking around I saw that the door was unlocked on my side.

"After everything gets settles, I'm going away for a while. I'll be on my beach in Bora Bora. Rest and relaxation is the key to success you know Mr. Tillis."

"I'm more than..." Blows from my fists was hitting Lance as hard as they could, anger blurring my vision.

"Asshole!"

"Stop it!" Lance yelled trying to shield his face, but I kept it up. I heard Spells tell the driver, "Pull over there and shut her up. I'm trying to enjoy the ride." Before we got over to the side of the road I punched Lance as hard as I could in the gut and lurched forward, opening my door and jumping out. I rolled in the grass and weeds along the side of the road then got up and ran, dizzy from the fall. I didn't stop, stumbling along the way. I could hear the car screeching to a halt. Spells was yelling. I bolted for the trees and instead of running straight into woods I ran along the shoulder, hoping someone would drive by and stop. Behind me I heard a gunshot, then another. I kept running, branches slapping me. I could hear movement but I didn't look back, too scared. The breath was on my neck, hot and searing.

Please God, don't let me die, I pleaded as I kept running, I could hear someone getting closer. I thought I had been running fast, but because I was so out of sorts from jumping out of the car, I didn't get too far. A hand grabbed my shoulder and pulled me down to the ground. I fell hard, the side of my head hitting the ground with a thud. I was flipped over and a large body was looming over me.

"You know the great thing about being out here." He grabbed my throat and started to squeeze.

"I can throw you away and no one will find you for days," he spat. I could only see a shadow just like in my dream. My head was spinning and I was beginning to lose consciousness. Before I blacked out his grip suddenly loosened on me. The last thing I remember was hearing a voice.

"This will be the last time we meet up."

♫

When I came to, I could hear Lance begging me to wake up. Slowing sitting up, I could see Spells was on the ground motionless. Once my mind cleared more, I scrambled away trying to get up.

"Stay away from me!" I was still dizzy and couldn't move as fast as I wanted to. It seemed like my body was in slow motion. He came closer.

"I'm not going to hurt you, Maxie." I cringed when he touched me. Lance looked me over, I could feel scratches up and down my arms, my shirt and pants were torn in places.

"Please Maxie." He touched my face and turned me to him. I could see a worried expression on his face.

"I'm so sorry." Spells was stirring and Lance rushed up and hit him in the back of the head to knock him out again. When he realized he wasn't getting up anytime soon he lowered his gun and came over to me.

"The police will be here any minute to get Spells, and FGA will be all over the place we have to go."

"What?" Lance lifted me off the ground gently.

"You have a concussion. Let me take care of you."

"Put me down, I'm not going anywhere!" I struggled but it was no use, he held me tighter.

"The only thing Spells knows is that he was running after you, he doesn't know what I did." I heard sirens in the distance. I kept moving, but he just held me tighter. I was hitting him, my head spinning more with every movement.

"You lied to me Lance, you lied! How could you!" He just held me and I kept at it, but he wouldn't let go.

"Put me down dammit! Listen to me!" It was like I was talking to a brick wall as he carried me over to the truck. Lance gently put me on the seat, then tried to reach out for me.

"You can still trust me." I snatched my arms away. I was mad, but beyond that Lance hurt my heart and nothing would change that.

"Tell me something, were your feelings for me a lie too?" I stammered. My face was hot with tears. He opened his mouth to speak but I stopped him.

"You know what, I don't want to know, it hurts too much already." I choked out. I looked through blurry eyes and saw the driver on the ground face down. Lance went over to Spells, tying him up with some kind of cord. Sitting in the truck, my head was at a dull ache. How could I have been so stupid? He sucked me right in and screwed me over. I had nowhere to go but with him and I didn't want to because I didn't know what the truth was. Nothing made sense to me. *He's been working with Meek this whole time and undercover in FGA? Or was it the other way around? He took Spells down so what does that mean? What about me, what's going to happen to me?*

My head was pounding; I was lightheaded and the scratches on my body burned. Lance was running back to the car. He jumped in, turned it around and headed back to the cottage, the one place I didn't want to go back to. He kept looking over at me as we drove along the couple of miles back. I kept staring straight ahead, my eyes were fuzzed with anger and tears.

"I'll explain everything when we are safe." Lance said after a couple minutes, I snorted.

"Safe? Are you kidding me? You call this safe?"

"Don't say that." We made it up the driveway, the garage door opening.

"Say what Lance? What the hell am I supposed to say! I don't know what to think. How am I supposed to act? Everything that I thought was a lie? Are you going to hand me over to them?" Hot tears were streaming down. "Who are you?" Lance looked at me tiredly. I felt pressure along my forehead, it was horrible. Lance got out and carried me inside, sitting me down on the couch.

"I just want to go to sleep, leave me alone." He cradled my head in his hands and looked at me caringly.

"I can't let you do that little lady." He told me that he had to keep me up for a while to make sure it wasn't a severe concussion. In the meantime, he cleaned up my scrapes and in the middle of that, decided to spill the sugar. Through the dizziness, I heard the whole story.

"My first big assignment was to take down some local drug dealers in Arizona. An ordinary task that turned into a bigger problem. These dealers were handling product for Meek, which we had no idea existed. The more we dug, the more we uncovered."

"It was my chief's idea to put me undercover to tear them inside out. Because of all my past experiences, I was the better fit. For month's I got higher up in rank and won trust in Spells. They had a lot more technology in staying under the radar than we expected so I agreed to still be undercover with Meek but give them the idea that I could infiltrate FGA so that Spells would think Meek would be always one step ahead of them. I kept FGA in the loop always and made sure he had no clue of the double cross."

If I believed everything that he said, that was a smart move on his and FGA's part. Get someone close on the inside get enough evidence then crush them. No holds barred at that point. Lance continued.

"My intention was to get to Mr. Bate's store that day before them and run surveillance. I knew something went wrong with the shipment and they were heading to see him. I was updating my chief and had told Spells that I couldn't ride with his associates there because it would be too close. By the time I got there it was too late. I wasn't expecting that and I wasn't expecting you." I rubbed my head, things made sense, but they didn't. This was too much.

"Why were you fighting the men in the park, why not talk to them and run them off?"

"Because, the men out here don't know me, never seen me and I was in full FGA mode. I couldn't risk switching. I was in too deep with both groups. When you came into the picture I knew that would be the final straw that hit with Meek because you witnessing what you did would no doubt help a grand jury convict. That's why I was put on full protection duty of you, to make sure nothing would get in the way of you being able to testify."

I thought about something Spells said when I overheard them talking and I couldn't remember Lance explaining it to me.

"Spells said something about men and when we were fleeing? No one ever followed us up here." Lance shook his head sadly.

"We were followed...the medicine I gave you knocked you out for a while. You never knew and I didn't tell you because I didn't want to scare you more than you already were. I took care of them." *That's why he kept saying he made sure we were safe at the cottage, it all made sense now.* I didn't ask any more on that because I didn't want to know what he did to them. My head pounded even more than before.

"I'm sorry Maxie I wasn't honest with you on this. It was a big burden and you didn't need it. Trying to be an agent and associate of Meek and protect..." I put my hand up and shook my head. My mind was spinning; I just didn't want to hear any more.

"Bullshit, you could have told me some kind of something instead of leading me on Lance. Who was I gonna tell, huh? Nobody! This hurts, this hurts bad." I slowly got up and I kept hobbling to the stairs. Helping me up there, he didn't say a word. We made it to my room and I stood in the doorway blocking him. His eyes were pleading with me, I had to look away. I slowly shut the door with my head down. Limping over to the shower, the water burned all the cuts on my arms. I stood with my head down trying to process everything.

I understood why Lance didn't tell me what was going on but I didn't. I mean I knew that me being a stranger, he couldn't trust me with information like that. On the other hand, once we got closer, I felt like I had the right to know.

I stayed in the shower until the water stopped stinging my cuts and got cold. I dried myself off and changed. Opening the door to see Lance was sitting on the bed. He had a first aid kit and had changed into some fresh clothes. He stood up as I crippled my way out and he helped me sit down. My body was beginning to stiffen up. It almost felt like the first time he brought me here and tended to me. He put my foot gently on his lap looked it at. There was some swelling but he wrapped it up and left it on his lap. I cleaned all my cuts up and as he was beginning to put band aids on all of them. I didn't want to say anything to him, but I did because I wanted him to know how I felt.

"I threw myself out there because you said over and over again I could trust you. I finally did and now I see you kept stuff from me. I never kept anything from you, Lance. Not one time and all along you were lying. Were you even going to tell me at all what was going on?"

"That's why I decided to end it all today. Because I wanted to end this, you didn't deserve any of it and it was eating at me. I care about you a lot Maxie, so I made some calls days ago and headed Spells in this direction. I contacted FGA and told them what was going to happen and they went into action. I planted a tracker but before that, I already put a microphone on myself. FGA heard everything Spells said. When you hit me and jumped out that was all I needed to make my move so you actually helped the plan work. Once Spells went after you I took care of the driver. I wouldn't have let anything happen to you I swear." Lance moved hair from my face.

"I thought it was the right thing to do." We sat there in silence, me pondering over everything Lance told me. He had good intentions, but shitty results.

"Is there anything else you need to tell me that you failed to mention?" Lance looked and me and blinked, after all this admission he actually looked embarrassed which threw me for a loop. He took a deep breath and rubbed his temples.

"When you talked to your parents the first time and you wanted me to stay with you, you were talking in your sleep that night."

"Ok..."

"You said you didn't want me to leave you and you were scared." A knot formed in my throat, something about that seemed familiar.

"When I told you I wasn't going to leave, you... kissed me." That was the dream I thought was so realistic. So, it was more realistic than I thought.

"Why didn't you tell me?" Lance stared at me.

"A part of me wanted to, but another part of me was selfish and wanted to have that memory to myself, even if you didn't remember." I thought about that dream and how I felt in it. I never told him about it myself so I couldn't really fault him, even though my end was a dream and his was a reality.

I looked closely at Lance and sighed deeply. I didn't realize he had a cut along the side of his arm until he turned to put the antiseptic down. I grabbed it and with my foot still on his lap, I cleaned it and bandaged it up. He also had a small cut along his hairline on his forehead. I put my foot down and moved closer to inspect it. It wasn't a deep cut but it was enough to spill blood. I was wiping it up when I heard Lance speak.

"Nothing about how I feel about you was fake." I stopped and stared at him blankly before I started cleaning his cut. He softly grabbed my hand staring me right in the eyes.

"Do you hear me? Nothing I felt was fake." I tried to keep my face stone but couldn't. I stared down at the floor trying not to show emotion.

"I'm sorry, I'm so sorry Maxie." I got up and hobbled to the window and sat on the chaise staring out for a long time, thinking about everything. Lance came over to me and stood looking out in the same direction. I couldn't bite my tongue anymore.

"You just don't do that to someone, leading them on like that. How am I supposed to forgive something like this, how am I supposed to trust something like this?"

Lance suddenly hugged me. I could hear him apologize over and over and say how he didn't mean to hurt me. He sounded defeated, he sounded, genuine. I could feel him relax a little because I didn't resist. The anger and pain that I had been feeling since the revelation was slowly diminishing, not completely, but some. He was doing his job, I told myself, he was trying to protect me, I said. I pulled away, I needed time.

Gray skies opened enough for a steady downpour. It was almost as if the weather knew my mood at that moment. I couldn't hear anything but the drops of water falling on the trees and grass. I finally turned and looked at him, the pain and dizziness in my head was just about gone. Lance grabbed my hands in his and slowly pulled me closer. He was trying to read my face.

"Did you even care enough to think about me in all of this?"

"I always cared...more than you knew," he replied.

"No, you didn't." He leaned forward, moving just inches apart from me. I could see his face.

"Yes, I did, and I still do." I could see the pain he felt, the regret. This was Lance, this was the man I wanted to see, the truth. I put a hand on his face and I looked in his eyes. Hesitantly, he kissed me; I closed my eyes. I felt his lips again.

"I promise I care," I heard him say. And that was when I realized that my feelings for him were stronger than I thought. We looked at each other and this time when our lips connected, I felt more than just a kiss, I felt what he said. I returned every one he gave me, they kept getting more and more intimate than the next. Lance picked me up and in between kisses, walked towards the bed, gently putting me down.

This was not supposed to happen. I was mad and I was hurt and I didn't know what to think, but yet this moment had been in my mind since the first time he kissed me. Now none of that mattered. I could see him pleading with his eyes for me to forgive him.

I felt his lips lightly on me. I could feel myself moving closer to him. Lance eased his body over me. He looked in my eyes and I touched him, kissing him deeply as we fell more.

"Do you?" I asked. He responded by tracing my face softly with his fingers. I sighed deeply, I knew his answer. I could feel full lips on my neck, my shoulders, and my collarbone. His hands gently felt the buttons and opened my shirt and he kissed every exposed area of my skin to my navel. My back arched and I moaned softly.

Coming back up, Lance kissed to the tops of my breasts; his hands floated to my thighs that I wrapped around his waist. I raised his shirt off, bare skin touching as our bodies pressed together. I was aching for him, and he was aching for me. You could see the fire in our eyes. When we gave ourselves to each other, nothing mattered but that moment in time.

I forgot about all the reasons why I was so mad earlier. I had been wanting this and there were so many times where we could have gone there, but we didn't. This time, we didn't stop, we both wanted this and nothing was going to stop that. All the feelings that we had both had were all out there now and there was no going back after this.

We both slept in each other's arms and the nightmares were nonexistent. When I woke up, Lance was still asleep. I grabbed a sheet, wrapped myself in it and eased downstairs to the piano. I had forgotten my ankle was wrapped so I made sure to sit so it would be raised. I stared outside. I could smell rain and within minutes a steady downpour came. The mist and a gentle breeze come through the screen.

I ran my fingers over the keys and my mind went out. This day had been a rollercoaster but ended without a malfunction. I felt good and I didn't think anything would ruin the moment. I was in a daze thinking about the man who turned my world upside down in a short matter of time. Everything I had felt prior to this with Lance, just amplified by a hundred.

I played for what seemed like hours before Lance came into the room and sat next to me. He sat in silence watching me play. I had no particular song in mind, I just played a melody I heard in my head. It flowed out like I had known it for years and I played it like I wanted people to feel what I felt. I saw reds and blues, cerulean, ivory and the tones kept coming. I eased out of it and looked over at Lance.

"I need you to promise me something."

"Anything," he said kissing my shoulder.

"Please be honest with me from here on out. I know why you did what you did, but it would have been easier if you would have told me. I don't want any more secrets."

"I promise." I paused for a moment, thinking of my words carefully as I spoke again.

"This is going to be hard Lance."

"Why?"

"Because when the time comes, I'm not gonna want to let you go."

Lance

Lance felt horrible. The thing he thought he could keep from her was now out. Not only did she know what he did when they were fleeing from the guys tailing them, but she knew now that he and Spells knew each other from another time. The look on her face he would never forget, it was of shock and pain. Maxie never had any reason to lie to him and there were many times he wanted to tell her, but he thought it was protecting her by not disclosing that information.

Lance and Spells had been working together for some time. He was helping run a weapons exchange while still working undercover. As the bust went down with FGA, one of the agents ran interference before Lance gave the call that Spells got away.

They fled and went separate ways with Lance going back to FGA until the chief told him it was time to lure Spells in. Lance contacted him with information that FGA was going to try and make some moves.

As far as Lance knew Spells was still in hiding, that is until Lance started putting pieces together. It started with Maxie describing the driver of the car that chased her down.

Then there was the mysterious car on her block after they fled to the cottage. Because there was never any proof of Spells reappearing, he had to do some digging to see if this was truly him, which it was. The closer he and FGA got to finding out where Spells was, the looser his grip changed on the situation. Lance decided the best way to end it was to trap Spells.

Lance could see the pain in Maxie's face when she realized what was going on. The truth was he never told her the part of the story where he was working with Meek and FGA as a double agent. It pained him to see her react to his touch. Even more so when she said he hurt her. How he could rewind back and tell her some of the story, at least then he could explain why he couldn't tell her anything. The ultimate sacrifice some would say is that the truth hurts to the core sometimes, even with good intentions.

He understood because he would have been upset too if someone he trusted his life with wasn't being honest. It would make you question everything they said afterward. Lance wanted her to know that he wasn't doing it other than to protect her from unpleasantness. There wasn't anything he wouldn't do for this woman and he wanted to prove it and he didn't know how, other than to show her. They had been somewhat close before on an occasion but not as intimate as they did that day.

Maxie

Eugene Spell was dying, at least that's what the prosecuting attorneys advised FGA. He was diagnosed with stage four lung cancer and only had a short time left.

"I guess karma really is a bitch," he quoted before pleading guilty to all charges. Whatever information they got from him must have been the mother lode because the next thing we knew, areas were raided and arrests were being made left and right in Mexico and Texas. Truckloads of product was confiscated and all the drugs were destroyed.

FGA had more than enough to take the whole group down with nothing left behind thanks to Spells. He had to be put in a special holding unit because he was now a target to the inside as a rat. It didn't make sense that this hardcore man would just decide to throw in the towel because he was dying. He didn't seem like the type of person with a conscious like that.

With Spells in custody and Meek down to the bare minimum, they were one hundred percent certain I could go home. They only knew we were in South Carolina because of the tag Lance gave Spells when he put his plan into action.

With the lead investigator being able to close the case, I was excited but nervous at the same time because I had been gone for over a month. Honestly, this place grew on me and so did something else, Lance.

There was no need to pack because neither one of us had come with anything to begin with so I cleaned everything up that I could. Afterward I stood out on the porch leaning on the railing. Smiling, I stepped down and out in the grass I walked along all the flowers all the way to the crab apple trees then opened the gate and kept going until I reached the hillside.

I tilted my head back and took a deep breath. It was finally over. All the terror was over. No more looking over my shoulder. No more wondering who was gonna come through that door. It was over.

Six weeks and two days ago, I was carried in here. Six weeks and two days ago, we were strangers. Things can sure change in such a short time. I got on the emotional roller coaster and felt like I wasn't going to finish the ride at times. *Strangers, enemies, friends, enemies, lovers, is that even how it's supposed to work?*

"Look at you," a voice from behind said.

"Look at me," I smiled back. I closed my eyes and felt the saltwater breeze on my face.

"So it's almost over little lady." I looked at the beautiful scenery and stopped at the endless sky. I looked over and smiled.

"Yes, it is." The weight that I had been wearing this whole time felt lighter and I was relieved. There was just one thing I needed to do to make it all go away.

"I need to see my parents."

"You know," he said kissing me, "We could stay one more night."

"Mmm, as tempting as that sounds, I still have my life back in Texas and you have yours. We have been gone a while. I'm sure my boss thinks I quit by now."

"So what now?"

"I don't know." Things were complicated as it was, adding a relationship as much as I wanted to the mix changed the flavor all together. But, maybe this would be over quicker than we thought. With no one being attached to a case anymore, it could work. I thought for a moment. Would I be able to wait if it's longer? That was the question that neither one of us knew how to answer.

♬

Mama and Daddy's house was actually a doublewide trailer on thirty acres of land. Cows lazily grazed in the distance and a huge garden with all kinds of fruits and vegetables laid in front of them. A deep green grass surrounded the house and Mama had lilacs next to the front door and a large corn field was spread out in the back. We took four steps up to a white screen door. Hummingbird wind chimes that matched mine at home twinkled with the gleaming sun. Opening the screen, I knocked on the wood door. I could hear footsteps shuffling along the floor.

Mama, wearing a blue sleeveless dress was the spitting image of myself twenty years from now. High cheek bones, smooth brown skin and shapely build, everyone thought we were sisters. Her curly black hair was now cropped in a short bob with strands of gray highlighting the front. I always thought she was the prettiest lady in Texas.

"Honey Bee!" Mama exclaimed. I was swallowed up in her arms.

"Hi Mama," I said tears welling up.

"Baby Girl is that you?" Daddy stepped from the front room to the door. Daddy was about 6'4, 250 and built like an ox. He played football when he was younger and still looked like he could put you on your pockets. He scooped me up in a huge bear hug. We stood there chatting and I completely forgot Lance was there until I saw something shift to the left.

"Oh my goodness, where are my manners, Lance these are my parents Karen and David McHill. Mama, Daddy, this is Lance Tillis. They all greeted each other, and Mama moved to the side so we could come in. A small room was filled with plants and pictures, there was only a sofa and an oversized recliner, with an ottoman in front of it. We sat down on the sofa with Lance on my right and Mama on my left holding my hand. Daddy was in the oversized chair, he turned off the T.V. then leaned back.

"I'm takin since you're here that you can go home now," Daddy said looking at Lance.

"Yes sir," I nodded. "No more Witness Protection."

"I'm so glad Honey Bee, we've been getting worried cause it's been so long." I looked over at Lance.

"I was well taken care of."

"Is that so?" Daddy inquired looking squarely at him.

"I can assure you, sir, I made sure of it." Mama grabbed my hand and lifted it up.

"I'm making supper for ya'll, you look starved doesn't she David?"

"No. If baby girl's hips spread anymore, she might be bearing children." His laugh boomed through the house as he sat up and slapped his leg.

"Daddy!" Mama got up and pulled me with her as she walked by. She hit Daddy in the arm and I stuck my tongue out at him. Lance laughed.

The small kitchen was to the left of the family room in an open square shape. The sink and short counter with cabinets below faced the back of the unit. A window above it looked out to a small corn field. The stove and oven were on a short wall, the small white refrigerator covered with magnets and pictures was next to it. Beyond that with a long wood planked hallway had a bathroom two bedrooms.

Mama grabbed bowls and flour, seasonings and chicken breasts out of the fridge. I knew Mama well, and I knew that she was bustling around because she was nervous and keeping her mind off the obvious, me being away for so long. My mouth watered as I knew she was going to prepare my favorite: smothered chicken fried steaks. I immediately grabbed fresh green beans and cleaned them.

I could hear Daddy asking Lance if he ever saw a double gas grill before. I turned and saw them walking out the front door. Moments later they appeared in the view of the back window. Daddy was in full 'look what I got' mode. I could see him lifting the top and opening all the compartments of the grill. Lance was nodding his head and looking on. I tapped on the glass and they looked up at me. Lance smiled showing his deep dimples and winked at me just as Mama came over to rinse off her hands. She peered out.

"That's a mighty fine young man there Honey Bee." She nudged my arm.

"He's not sore on the eyes that's for sure," I said. Mama looked at me then at Lance and moved back to the counter. I finished with the green beans and poured them into a pot of water on the stove. I added seasonings and Mama came over with some raw bacon that I crumbled on top. I always loved cooking with her.

"Are y'all gonna drive thru or stay tonight and head out in the morning." I washed my hands in the sink.

"I'm not ready to go back home right away, so if we stay tonight is that okay?" Mama wiped her hands on her apron.

"Of course sugar...I'm so glad you're ok. Mamas been worried rabbits about you." She came and kissed my cheek and squeezed my shoulder. "Now go on now and save that poor man from your daddy, I'll be fine in here." She shooed me out the kitchen.

I walked out the front door, down the steps and around to the back. Daddy and Lance were still standing beside the grill, and he was explaining to Lance how he got a good steal on it.

"You seem like the type of man that knows what I'm talkin bout now. The gals don't understand, even if I save $3 it's better than $3 more." I walked right up to Daddy and put my hand around him with my head barely touching the top of his shoulder.

"Now you know Daddy, if you're gonna talk about the grill you should probably show Lance how a real cook can grill some sweet corn." Daddy snapped his fingers.

"Baby girl, I like your thinkin." He pecked the top of my forehead.

"We can go pick some out." Daddy held up his hand.

"You know I gots to pick em. Ya'll don't never get the sweet ones. Gon now, I can't be showing my secrets."

The half an acre yard away stood a huge pecan tree and a plum tree. The pecan tree had a wooden swing hanging from its branches and a picnic bench that was just under the shady leaves. I sat on the swing and Lance got behind to push me.

"So did your dad make this?" I nodded.

"He said when they have grandbabies he can give the proper crash course in swinging." I laughed. "If you hadn't noticed already, he's a character."

"Do you want kids?"

"Yeah, I would love to have kids one day, what about you?" Lance continued to push me on the swing softly.

"I never really thought about it, but I think I probably would."

"Why do you say it like that?"

"The way I work it wouldn't be good if I had kids right now. My profession is unpredictable as you can see." I felt the warm breeze on my skin and thought about what he said as I kicked my legs out slowly.

Mama and Daddy would be tickled pink and spoil them like crazy. I smiled to myself and slowed to a stop. Lance moved away and sat at the picnic table. I stared at the plum tree then jumped off the swing. Plucking off one, I walked over to Lance with it. Taking a bite, I put it in front of him to taste, then sat next to him looking out at the crops.

"Do you ever think about leaving FGA and doing something else?" I asked.

"Sometimes, but I don't know what I would do instead." I took another bite then put it back in front of him, Lance grabbed my hand.

"I want to ask you something."

"Okay." He seemed a little hesitant and even nervous so I thought it must be important.

"Things will be pretty crazy when we get back and I'll be all over the place, but I want to see you. Is that ok?"

"Yes." I was so glad to hear Lance say that, so glad because I as beginning to think about what I would do after all of this was over. I leaned forward and touched his lips as he pulled me in.

"I'm so glad you said yes, I think I should get you on that trip with me to Morocco after all."

♫

Mama made smothered chicken fried steaks, mashed potatoes, green beans, macaroni and cheese, and biscuits. Daddy grilled his famous sweet corn and I was in heaven.

We sat at the picnic table under the pecan tree. Mama was across from Daddy and I was across from Lance. Once he asked Lance if he watched football, the men were in their own little world and we became invisible.

From time to time I would catch him looking at me. I'd smile at him and he'd smile back. I didn't know Mama noticed these exchanges until she nudged me.

"I can see that you know," she whispered. I looked at her in surprise.

"Chile, how didn't I know, I'm your mama. Come with me to get this pie." We gathered up the empty plates and walked into the house. I put my dishes in the sink and walked over to grab the pie out of the fridge. Mama blocked my path and crossed her arms.

"Spill the sugar." I leaned back on the counter and sighed.

"It just happened Mama. We were in that place for so long and got to know each other alot. I don't think either one of us was lookin for it." I picked at a small chip on the counter.

"I really like him." Mama looked at my face, her arms slowly unfolded.

"And what about him." I smiled at her.

"He likes me a lot too." Mama turned and got the pie out the fridge.

"Well then, I won't ask no more of it. If you both like each other, ok then." I gave her a hug and she laughed it off. "Now let's feed those two good looking men out there." Making our way back outside, Mama put the pie on the table. I laid the saucers next to it.

"Yes indeed! Young man, you gots a treat on your hands right here." I served the pie and we sat watching the sun move through the trees.

This is real good," Lance remarked finishing his piece. I ate every crumb on my plate and licked my fork, everyone staring and laughing.

"I think I need another slice."

Mama and Daddy insisted they clean up while Lance and I grabbed some things from the truck. We walked back in and I lead Lance down the hall and to the right. The small room held a full-size bed, one dresser drawer, a night stand and a small T.V. There were pictures of music notes along the wall. A keyboard was underneath a small window that overlooked the cornfield.

"So this must be your room." I smiled and nodded. He was walking around the looking at the notes when Daddy walked by.

"Y'all get settled in?"

"Yes, sir."

"We headin to bed now, y'all get yourself together and breakfast is first thing." I gave him a hug and he nodded.

"Night Daddy."

"Night Baby Girl…Big L. I turned and looked at Lance.

"Mr. McHill." Daddy walked down the hall and I closed the door.

"Big L?" Lance shrugged his shoulders and I sat on the bed giggling. He looked at me and laughed.

"I like your parents; they seem pretty down to earth."

"Yeah, they've always been like that. Don't let my daddy fool you though, he can be a bear if he needs to."

"I'm sure of that." Lance sat down next to me and we talked for a long time, mostly about me and what it was like growing up.

"I heard you talk about your grandma a lot. It sounds like you two were close." I nodded my head and smiled.

"We were two peas in a pod. Every chance I got, I would come visit and we would sit and snap peas or hang clothes or something around this place. She was old school and wasn't into all the technology, said it was too fancy to her liking. I used to sit and listen to her talk about when she was younger and how things were so different these days."

"She sounded like a gem," Lance replied.

"She really was. Gram taught me the true feeling of playing the piano too. Sure, I had classes and all that, but she made me feel what I was playing, know what I mean? I sure miss her. She was eighty-five when she passed in her sleep one night. Even though we took it hard, I think she was ready. She used to tell us all the time that she had no regrets, except Kolby Knots back in 51'. 'Chile, he was slick as oil on the fingertips. He tried to get fresh with me and clocked him in the nose. I wish I hit him with something else.'" We laughed and got ready to go to bed.

I got under the covers and faced Lance. *I could get used to this every night*, I was telling myself. He leaned in and kissed me, and I returned it, letting it linger.

"Good night little lady." I kissed him one more time.

"Good night Lance." I turned around and he cradled me until I dozed off.

Morning came quickly. Mama made eggs, sausage links, toast with plum jelly and bacon with coffee. Afterward, we grabbed our things and headed to the truck. We had some hours before I got home. Daddy gave me a hug and kissed my cheek then he shook hands with Lance.

"Thanks for keeping my baby girl safe," I heard him say. Mama came over with tears in her eyes to embrace me.

"Call me as soon as you get home Honey Bee."

"I will Mama." I got in the seat and Lance climbed into the driver side. He looked over at me.

"Ready?"

"Yeah." We both waved as the truck pulled away. I directed Lance to the freeway and we made our journey back to my house. About halfway into the trip, I started thinking about my time away from home and the growing relationship between the two of us. Everything about it sounded right. Lance looked over and grabbed my hand.

As we approached my house, anxiety kicked in. All the bad memories flooded in my mind. I seized up and clutched the door handle. There was a car parked out in the front of the house. A white man, short, thick and bald, he had a cigarette hanging from his mouth and his arms crossed. His dark gray suit fit nicely, but his tie was loosely around his neck. I could see him pat his brow with a handkerchief.

"Maxie?" My heart started racing. Lance grabbed my hand and rubbed it back and forth.

"The men in the house." He leaned over cupped my chin.

"Everything was taken care of long ago," he said soothingly. He told me to take some deep breaths. After a few, I got myself together.

"Ok?" I nodded and he kissed my lips lightly. When he got out the car, the man had uncrossed his arms they met up in front of the truck. I couldn't hear anything, but Lance was doing most of the talking. The man patted his head with his scarf. I slowly got out of the car and approached them.

"Ms. McHill, I'm Chief Deputy Rowlan with FGA. We met briefly in the hospital." I shook his hand lightly and looked at my house.

"Tillis, I need you at down at the office by 3pm. We need to get you up to speed with things." He looked at me for a moment. "And you need to bring me up to speed on things too." I turned and walked up my sidewalk to my front door. Turning my key slowly I walked in and stood there, glancing around. Everything was just as I had left it, it was as if nothing happened here. I walked down the hall and stopped. I had to blink a couple of times to realize no one was there. I had been holding my breath and didn't blow the air out until I heard Lance behind me and touch my shoulder.

"It feels so weird being here." Lance looked around before he spoke.

"It probably will be for a while." We walked in each room inspecting it. They did a good job making sure no trace of anything was left. I made it into my piano room and stood in front of it. I traced my fingers over the keys, it felt good.

"Will you be ok while I head in for a couple of hours?"

"I think so."

"Ok, let me get going. I'll be back soon ok." My mind was going fast.

"Hurry back," I said.

"Absolutely."

I walked him back to the door and watched him leave. I turned and looked around again, it really was like nothing had happened. I made sure everything was locked up, then I climbed the stairs.

Sitting on the bed, I grabbed my phone and called Mama. Daddy picked up on the second ring.

"Hey baby girl, you made it home ok?"

"Yes, sir."

"Good, good. Look here, we're gonna come down that way in a couple days to see some friends so me and Mama will see you then. I want to put some extra locks on your stuff too."

Thanks Daddy. I'm gonna go now I'll see you soon." We hung up and I fell back on my bed looking at the ceiling, my mind going back to Lance. You would think that being with someone day and night for weeks at a time would be tiresome, but it wasn't. The truth was that I now think the best way to get to know someone is to hunker down with them for days at a time. If you don't feel a connection after being that close to someone for that long, then it's not meant to be.

I sat up and showered and for the first time in weeks, besides at my parents, I put my own clothes on, and it felt good. Heading into the kitchen I opened the fridge and it was empty. Thank goodness because everything would have been beyond expired and sour like day old milk and cream on the counter. I decided then and there that I needed to get out and get some fresh air, I didn't want to stay cooped up. I had done enough of that already.

I got in my car and forgot that it still wasn't working. Getting out, I grabbed my purse and walked into town. It was only a couple of blocks to Ties Street which was the main street and from there only another eight blocks to get to the store. If I walked west for a mile, I'd run into the lounge. I decided to go there first.

The walk was just what I needed. Hearing the birds chirping and cars passing by and people walking around, it felt almost normal. I didn't realize how isolated I had been these past weeks. My thoughts of Lance slowly faded into the back of my mind when I walked into the bar and saw a familiar face. Tyler Bets was talking to a waiter and stopped mid-sentence when he saw me.

"Maxie, my darling!" He hugged me so tight I thought he broke a rib.

"It's good to see you too Tyler." I laughed at his gesture. I pulled out of my purse a huge bag of jelly beans I made Lance get when we were coming back from my parents. Tyler's face lit up like a child getting a five-dollar bill but then he pulled from me uncertainty on his face.

"You're back, right?"

"Yes." He hugged me again and I laughed.

"Oh thank goodness, honey you have no idea. It hasn't been the same with you gone."

We spoke for a few moments then I walked around and greeted all the staff. Once I spotted the piano I walked over to it. Frowning I saw an empty glass on the top. Only one person I knew did that.

"Jerry! What the hell man, I leave for a little bit and you act like you own my piano. I told you last time I was gonna kick your ass if you didn't clean up after yourself." Everyone turned and pointed to the back room. Jerry Stiles came rushing out. About 5'10 and one hundred and thirty pounds soaking wet, Jerry was skawny to me but had a little swag to him that all the ladies seemed to enjoy when he played. He and I worked together since I started at the lounge years ago. We always bickered back and forth and it made entertainment for everyone who worked there whenever we were in the same room. Jerry burst out the kitchen.

"Goddammit Maxie! Stop acting out in front everybody, you ain't the boss, ain't that right Tyler! And I told you I'll put my glass where I want!" He came up the stage and we stared each other down. Then we laughed and hugged each other. I didn't realize how much I missed my family here until that moment. I was so glad I decided to come in.

"Nice to see you, Max."

"You too, Jerry." I told him he would have to hold down the place for another day and then I'd be back.

"Take your time, I've been enjoying the extra tip nights, but let me say you missed it about a week ago with Miss Bertha."

"Oh hell, what did she do now?" Jerry started cracking up and I tuned in, ready for the gossip I so needed.

"Oh, she did it this time. Miss Bertha decided to have a little melt down outside in the parking lot cause Phil locked the keys in the car. She swung that purse so hard, almost knocked his block off his rocker. Tyler had to call the sheriff cause she wouldn't stop throwin stuff at him in the street. Had to spend a night cooling down in the cell."

Jerry got me all caught up on the happenings and I eased my way down to the bench and started tapping keys.

I played a couple bars on the piano and the staff including Tyler and Jerry egged me on to do a song. I finally caved and played an upbeat piece. Everyone came in the dining area to listen. Their bodies were moving with the beat, hands hitting each other. I got a loud applause and felt so happy I thought I would burst. I really missed my family here at Land's Down.

I spoke to a couple more people then headed out. Instead of going to the store, I figured Lance and I could order out for dinner. I started walking back home. I wasn't paying attention and went west instead of east. Fifteen minutes later, Surpent Park loomed ahead of me. The huge trees that I once loved to spend hours in now looked dark and gloomy.

I slowly walked up to the sidewalk entrance and looked around. No cars in sight. There were some kids coming down a plastic twisty slide as their parents looked on. The only happiness I'll probably have again here is the happiness I had when Lance found me hiding in that crawlspace hurt and scared. A shiver ran through my spine and I turned and headed back home.

♫

Lance came back to my house late that night. I ordered some takeout and while we waited I asked him what happened at the office.

"The chief didn't take too lightly I got personally involved with you. He saw us in the car earlier."

"Oh."

"So after I got put up to speed on things he told me I couldn't be on the case anymore. Conflict of interest."

"Shit, I didn't think of that," I remarked. This whole time I was more worried about how I was feeling and didn't even think of how our situation would affect everything.

"He can't do that. And you can't throw everything you worked to do with Meek away because of me." I felt horrible about this turn of events.

"Yes he can, he's the chief. I'll be fine." I stood and paced looking out the front window.

"This isn't your fault, I'm pretty sure neither one of us expected this to happen, but it did and this is the result of that."

"So what happens now?"

"What happens is that I turn in all information I have on Meek. I have to meet up with everyone in FGA that was involved with it and wait to see what the chief has for me next. I have to leave tomorrow to get started." I felt more horrible by the minute. I sighed deeply, Lance turned me to face him.

"I don't want you to hold this burden, I'm ok, besides being with you makes it worth it." He kissed me softly.

"Are you sure you're ok with not being a part of it anymore."

"I'm one hundred percent sure, but only if you promise you won't find someone else while I'm gone. Will you wait for me?"

"Of course."

"Even if it takes some time before I come back?" he kissed me again.

"Even if it takes some time before you come back," I replied.

Lance left late in the morning. I really hated to see him go but, I knew he had a lot of things to do before he could come back. We stayed in bed until Lance got up to shower and got ready. I laid there under the blanket thinking about the previous night and the fact that he would be gone for some time. My feelings were well beyond just infatuation and attraction; it was more than that. I realized I had fallen in love with Lance. I wanted to tell him but I didn't want to cloud his focus on what he needed to do.

He came out with a towel around his waist. His muscular chest was glistening and I was taking it all in. I leaned up on my elbow, the sheet clinging to my body.

"You sure you have to leave soon?" He laid on the bed and kissed me down to the pillow.

"Mmmm. Yeah, I do." Lance got up off the bed. I climbed out and showered while he got things together. When I got out, Lance was fully dressed and was grabbing his bag. We went downstairs. I made coffee and some food and we ate. Lance stared at me most of the time and I stared back. Finally, I spoke up.

"What's up?" He looked at me more and smiled. Lance motioned like he wanted to say something but instead got up.

"I better get out of here, lots to do and the quicker I get it done, the quicker I can get back to my little lady."

I got out of my chair and walked him down the hall and to the door. He opened it then turned and grabbed my face. That kiss sealed my feelings for real.

"Wow," I breathed. Lance smiled.

"Wow?"

"Yeah." He stepped on the porched and turned back.

"I'll call you in a few days, ok?" He walked to his truck got in and drove away. I stood in the doorway following the truck all the way down the street.

W. Owens

Lance

What about Maxie? Lance realized that he cared about her more than he realized and he was willing to leave his position to be with her. Lance didn't want to lose her. He knew that he was jumping the gun in more ways than one, but the thoughts continued to linger in the back of his mind as he went back to the office to talk to the chief.

Being at Maxie's parents' house and having time to think, Lance knew he wanted to have a real relationship with her, beyond this romance that came of them being together due to circumstance. He wanted nothing more than to spend even more time with the beautiful woman with the curly hair that lit up every room she walked in. It went through his mind as he watched her parents and thought about what would happen after they got back to Pine Forest, Texas.

Knowing that Maxie wanted to still be around him after the fact made Lance feel like his life was going in a good path, that is, until they got back.

Explaining to the chief what happened, Lance knew there would be repercussions to it, he just didn't know that he would have to make a choice between his job and Maxie. On

237

the drive back to Maxie's he thought about the pros and cons of it. If he stayed at the job, could he be satisfied with it, could he hate it? Would he be one hundred percent committed to whatever he was assigned to? By leaving the case he was beginning to tire from, he would have more time to spend with her, but what would he do? Would he pick up another case? Would he leave FGA all together? If things did work out with him and Maxie, Pine Forest was such a small town, would he even want to stay there? Where would he work? His cottage, he knew he wasn't going to get rid of no matter what. Memories he had stamped in his mind needed to not be disturbed.

Maxie

Mama and Daddy came to my house first thing in the morning. Daddy had a tool kit, an alarm system, window locks, and a chain to put on the front door.

"Daddy, I don't want to be trapped in here, geez do you have enough stuff."

"Don't you worry about that." He went to his pickup truck and came back with a security ladder to put at my bedroom window.

"Man at the store said this heres top of the line." I looked at Mama and threw up my hands

"Is this really necessary?" I asked. They both stared at me like they were gonna shake me to death. I slowly backed out of the room.

"Never mind I said that," I mumbled.

I grabbed bottle water and took a swig just as Mama came in the kitchen with the security ladder box. I grabbed it and took it upstairs with Mama following me. I unrolled it and pulled out the directions. The red ladder had curves at the top that fold over your window sill, there were no screws

239

or bolts or anything except a tote to keep it in. I rolled it back up and placed it right next to the window on the floor. Back downstairs Daddy was screwing the first lock in the window in my living room.

"See here," he said pointing to the lock. "It's a butterfly screw. All you do is place it as for open as you want the window to be and tighten it." He opened the glass about six inches then tightened the screw. He shut the window then opened it hard. It made a loud boom when it hit the lock.

"You can hear that all the way upstairs." I nodded, impressed with it. Daddy moved on to another window. I went to go cut some vegetables and fruit to put into the blender. Mama grabbed milk and frozen yogurt, chopping strawberries, and was talking about something but I wasn't listening. My mind was on the man who turned my world upside down without knowing it. It had been a week and I hadn't heard from Lance and I was starting to worry. Maybe he's busy. Or even worse, what if something happened to him? Maybe he changed his mind about me? I started thinking about Lance.

"You miss him don't you Honey Bee?" Mama must have picked up on my silence because she stopped talking and moved closer to me.

"I'm sure he'll come back soon baby." I looked back at her, sighed and put the knife down.

"But what if he doesn't, I mean what if he's finally got tired of me and all this shit…. sorry Mama." She crossed her arms like she always did when she wanted the truth.

"I fell in love Mama."

"And?" I was surprised that she did have a reaction to what I just told her.

"And, I don't know what to do."

"Honey Bee, it's not that hard, if you love him, you love him, simple as that. Y'all can figure out all the other stuff later. It works in mysterious ways you know. Give him some time, I'm sure he's busy. You guys were gone a long time baby. Besides, I know what I know and Honey bee, that man feels the same way." I picked up the knife and finished chopping up the fruit, glad Mama was there to help me calm it down in my mind.

After Mama and Daddy left, I called work and told them I wanted to pick up some more time which perked me up because that beat me moping around the house all day. I had been moody lately and I needed a change. Since I was in good spirits, I went to Gram's piano and sat there thinking I wanted to do something different tonight. Usually, the stage was set and depending on the night, we had a theme. Sometimes at the end of the set, I would freestyle to an audience pick. I didn't want to do that tonight.

I decided I wanted to play my story. Everything I went through I needed that flowing through my fingers. No one knew what happened, and no one needed to know but me. I sat there in silence, taking my memory back and let my fingers do the talking. It started with humming, then the words came out. The more I played, the more I liked where it was going. I grabbed my pen and paper with an idea.

Thursday nights was always fun because a local band would play the whole night with me. 410 was their names and they had a keyboarder, drummer, bass, saxophone player. The singer's name was Saphire and she was really good. I sang with her one night after we closed up for the night, and man we would have brought the house down. All the people that were working that night told us we needed to make a cd together.

As much as loved singing when I played, I usually kept that part of myself to myself, but every now and then it happens. I talked to the band and we decided that we would, well, I would perform on the last song of the night. I didn't tell Tyler because he's always begging me to do it so I was gonna give him a surprise as well. I got up to the chair and the band got ready.

"For our last piece of the night I wanted to do a little something I don't normally do. I hope you enjoy."

I sang that song like it was the last time I would be able to use my voice. I kept belting it out and the band followed suit. I even teared up at the end. When we finished, the crowd went off, they were all standing. Tyler was in the back throwing his hands up and all the wait staff was cheering. I took my bows and gave Saphire a hug because she was on point with the background vocals, like we rehearsed all day and night for it, even though we really didn't.

I got off the stage and a yellow tulip was placed in hands by one of the waitresses. Frowning, I leaned forward and called her back.

"Shawna! What's this for?"

"Girl, I don't know but this fine man told me to give it to you." She pointed to the back of the lounge.

I saw a silhouette by the exit sign and I just knew it was Lance. I got off the stage trying to get to him and was greeted by people telling me how good that was. A man approached me wearing a suit.

"Ms. McHill. I'm the manager at APlus music. I've heard some of your pieces on the radio and just loved them, but this one right here," he pointed to the stage, "I think any one of my artists would love to perform it. We need to talk soon." He handed me his card, and I was beside myself.

"Oh my goodness, thank you thank you! Yes, we will talk very soon." I shook hands and continued in the direction I saw Lance. He was nowhere to be found. I went out the back exit and looked down the alley and out into the street, nothing. I shook my head; I just knew I saw him but where was he? I looked once more look then walked back in the lounge. I must have been seeing things. When I got back inside, Tyler was on cloud nine.

"Miss Lady, I think you brought the house and all the buildings nearby down." He hugged me so hard he popped my back. I laughed.

"Ok, ok, I had a good set tonight."

"Girlie, that was better than good! I may have to start charging people covers to get in here and listen to you." A waitress gave me some lemon water and a small cloth to pat my brow. I went to my favorite spot and sat down, feeling the high off the atmosphere in there. People were still coming by and telling me how much they enjoyed that. It felt so good and I was really excited about the music executive. Looking down at the flower I placed on the table I looked around more. It just would have been even better if a certain someone would have stayed around long enough.

Lance

Lance thought about all those years he was out in the field fighting the bad guys, always being in the heat of danger. When he was young, it excited him but as he got a little older, he realized there was more in the world than just fighting the bad guys. His dad always taught him to 'know what you know' and what Lance knew was that he didn't want to be out there anymore.

Working alone gave you time to reflect and think about the future. He thought of his parents and how they had such a loving relationship. Thirty years, they had been married and never looked back. Now that his dad was gone, his mom to him looked lost, she had to be alone for whatever years she had left. He knew what it was like to feel like no one was there and you turn your shoulder, the space behind you is empty. He didn't want to spend the rest of his life like that. He had a big heart and wanted to share it with someone, the problem was, how could he?

He's never been in a serious relationship so he never went through what other couples did. Lance also never felt too strongly about a lady either. There were times he tried but there was never a 'connection' as his dad said. Sure, the women loved how he looked but it usually ended up being a fizz. This was the first time Lance ever felt something for a woman so strongly and because of this, he didn't want to let it go.

He wished so bad his dad was around to talk to him about it, but he wasn't. The time he has spent with Maxie was been under crazy circumstances, to say the least, but for some reason he can't stop thinking of her. The way she wears her hair, her face, the way her eyes crinkle up at the corners when she smiles. Those full lips of hers he catches glimpses of when she isn't looking.

Lance knew that his job as a Special Operative didn't include falling crazy on a witness, that was not in the handbook. Though he knew of the risks, he also knew that the lady with the beautiful eyes and soft southern drawl was something he wasn't sure he wanted to let go.

Maxie

I checked three times, and three times it came back the same. Pregnant! I sat on the edge of the bathtub in shock. *Pregnant!* For fifteen minutes I took test, after test, after test, sitting on my bed watching the clock tick down each time.

Peeking at the first one, it showed two blue lines. I read the box then looked back at the test. Shaking my head, I took another test and waited; that one came back with a plus sign. I read that box and then grabbed the last one. Within minutes it read *pregnant*.

"No, no, no, this can't be happening right now," I sobbed. *How could I not have paid attention to the signs earlier?*

A week after Lance was gone, I hadn't been feeling too well. I didn't think it was the flu because I wasn't getting really sick or had the hot cold flashes like I normally did with that. I just felt queasy and crampy, which to me was a normal monthly thing. I went on like I usually did, grabbing my popcorn with chocolate covered bites and got ready listen some blues records and writing sheet music. The scent of my favorite triple-buttered popcorn made me nauseous as soon as I smelled it out of the package and I dry heaved all the way down the hall. I spent two days in bed eating popsicles because that was all I wanted and I was so exhausted; like I hadn't slept in weeks.

Just as suddenly as I felt sick, I bounced right out of it and ate all day. My excuse was I was making up for the two-day popsicle binge. In the middle of stuffing a french fry in my mouth, a TV commercial came on for a diaper brand. I stared up at the cutest little baby and a mom cuddling her to death. I looked down at my stomach, imagining what it would be like to have something growing inside then my heart nearly stopped. Racing up to my room, I checked my personal calendar and realized my period was late, beyond late.

"Shit!" I grabbed my purse and rushed out the door.

I spent an hour pacing the floor, looking at each test and reading the boxes over and over again. I threw all but one away. *How am I supposed to tell Lance? Am I even ready for this?* The phone rang breaking my thoughts. The ID said it was unrestricted which told me it was Lance. I took a deep breath and answered, not knowing how to even start the conversation. As soon as the receiver clicked, I heard him yelling on the other end.

"Maxie, get out of the house!"

"What?"

"Get out of the house, Spells escaped the facility..." I dropped everything and grabbed my keys. Running down the stairs, I swung open my door and standing in front of me was Eugene Spells and a huge man that in one motion grabbed me. Before I could scream, my mouth was covered and I smelled something horrific. I could feel myself clawing at his hands even when everything went dark.

♫♪♩ ♫♪♩ ♫♪♩ ♫♪♩ ♫♪♩ ♫♪♩

W. Owens

Lance

I got to the townhouse as fast as I could through traffic. My heart was pounding, if Spells was going do anything, it would be to get Maxie. She was a threat and he had nothing to lose by taking her out. I was sure by now Spells knew my secret and would try to get to me. Maxie hadn't called me and it was worrisome because if she made it somewhere safe, she would have.

"Maxie!" Bursting through the door, nothing looked out of place. I went into each area downstairs, the living room, the piano room, bathroom, all the closets, and the kitchen. Everything was fine, the doors didn't even look like there was any forced entry. I ran to the back and checked the garage.

"Maxie!" her car was still there. Something wasn't right, I could feel it in my gut.

Going back into the house I found her keys on the ground next to a bush by the door and picked them up. They weren't hidden at all. I went back inside and looked at everything again before climbing the stairs.

"Maxie, Maxie! Answer me! I'm here!" Entering her room, I could see the dropped phone on the ground but there was something next to it. Picking it up I frowned, my frown turned into shock. I saw the words *Pregnant*. My phone rang loudly and I picked it up immediately.

"Maxie?" A smoky voice answered instead.

"What you don't realize Mr. Tillis, is that I have been doing this a lot longer than you have. Did you really think I wouldn't do my homework on you? I must say, you were very clever. Trying to be my right-hand man and making me believe you got in good with FGA when you were an agent all along. Very clever." Spells coughed into the phone.

"I'm pretty disappointed in you, you had so much promise, but, what's done is done. I'm sure you know by now I won't be on this earth too much longer so I decided that my final breaths will be to give you a challenge, I'm sure you'll figure out where we are, but hopefully it won't be too late. Say bye honey."

"Lance!" The phone went dead. Staring down, I could hear the tone blasting out the earpiece. My other hand held the plastic stick. *Pregnant!* I blinked thinking the words weren't really there, but they glared hard back. Maxie was pregnant, and Spells took her. My hands shook with anger as I dialed the chief to tell him what was going on.

"Spells has Maxie, I'm going after her."

"Now hang on a minute Tillis, you're off the case. I'll get the guys together; you get involved and I'll have to..."

"I'm already involved Chief, and if you think for one minute I'm going to sit back and watch, you must not know me that well." The chief was talking but I wasn't listening, I was looking around trying to find some clue, anything that would give me a hint as there where they were.

"Tillis...Tillis?! Do you hear me, don't you dare interfere." I hung up the phone and sat on the stairs putting my head in my hands. The place showed no signs of forced entry, everything was fine. I couldn't figure out what I was missing and frustration was building. My mind went to the back door where I found the keys on the ground. Standing up, I made my way to that spot and let my eyes wander. They rested on what looked like a balled up tissue in mulch. Looking closely, I used a pen and picked it up. The tissue was actually a piece of ripped thin cloth.

Before I had it to my nose the pungent smell of chloroform burned at my nostrils. The ground looked unsettled, but other than that, nothing was astray. *If the cloth was still damp, that means that this was pretty recent and if it was pretty recent, then they weren't too far away.* I thought to the phone call, there was no background noise except for Maxie when the phone cut off. That eliminates anything that moves so they couldn't be driving, they have to be in a room of sorts. I wasn't sure but I was going on a hunch as to where they may be.

Getting to the truck, my phone was ringing off the hook. The chief wasn't going to let it up.

"What?!" I said yelling in the receiver.

ABOUT THE AUTHOR

In my middle school and high school years, my journal was a way of telling stories. Each day, no matter how uneventful, something was always written down.

As years went on, my mind started picturing ideas and characters that I wanted to create, but never got around to painting them on paper.

Being a part of The Institute of Children's Literature and obtaining a certificate for writing Short Stories, finally put my spirits high to achieve the goal of becoming a writer.

I am currently working on another writing project and two short stories.